Middle
of
Nowhere

A girl holding a spanner came out of the machine room – a girl so sunburned, so unwashed and unbrushed, that he could not tell at first if she was European or Aboriginal, so thin and starved of sleep that her eyes were dark hollows. Greasy hair was screwed into a knot on top of her head and stuck through with two knitting needles. Her licked lips were like crumpled tissue paper, gummed at the corner with sores. Mr. Boyce put the pistol behind his back.

"Hello. I am Jack. I was at your parents' wedding. You must Comity."

USBORNE MODERN CLASSICS

iducing timeless stories to today's readers

Praise for
GERALDINE McCAUGHREAN
and
The Middle of Nowhere

Shortlisted for the Carnegie Medal
Winner of the Young Quills Award for Historical Fiction

"This novel about courage, love and tolerance sings with
McCaughrean's glorious, new-minted phrase-making."
The Sunday Times

"Geraldine McCaughrean writes a superb sentence, and
they come thick and fast in *The Middle of Nowhere*."
Booktrust

"Full of phrases, images and ideas that pull you up short,
and is a brilliant adventure too."
Books for Keeps

"A clear-sighted, beautifully written examination of
racism and courage."
Metro

GERALDINE McCAUGHREAN

The Middle of Nowhere

USBORNE MODERN CLASSICS

For Veronique and Laura, with love and thanks

Editorial consultant: Tony Bradman

This edition first published in the UK in 2018 by Usborne Publishing Ltd., Usborne House, 83-85 Saffron Hill, London EC1N 8RT, England. www.usborne.com

First published in 2013. Copyright © Geraldine McCaughrean, 2013

Cover illustration by Lucinda Puruntatameri, Munupi Arts and Crafts Association Inc. Copyright © Usborne Publishing Ltd

The name Usborne and the devices ♕ 🌐 are Trade Marks of Usborne Publishing Ltd.

A CIP catalogue record for this book is available from the British Library.

JFMAM JASOND/18 ISBN 9781409570516 02351/12

Printed in the UK.

CHAPTER ONE

Camels in the Yard

The piano arrived too late to stop the sky falling in. If it had come earlier, things might have ended on a sweet note. As it was, everything was jangled, unstrung, struck dumb.

Pestered by flies, Comity squatted beside the mound of red earth in the corner of the compound, watching ants explore the new upland in their landscape. How huge it must seem to them – how startling that the ground should have suddenly risen up, disturbing their nests, their sacred sites, their ant city.

"Take your shoes off your feet," she told them. "The place whereon you're crawling is holy ground."

The ants paid no attention. Four feet below the surface, Comity's mother lay wrapped in a sheep fleece, safe from dingoes or crows. By tomorrow, though, the ants would have searched her out and made her part of their underworld territory. Comity looked back at Telegraph House. The curtains were drawn. After the funeral, her father had fairly sprinted inside, slamming shut the door on the sunshine, the heat, the flies, the stockmen, the words of sympathy, the appalling truth. Today he had not set foot outside, not even to see the wooden grave marker someone had wedged into the mound:

Comity, on the other hand, was drawn time and again to this corner of the yard. She told herself that she was there to pray, because that is what people do at gravesides, isn't it? But part of her knew she was checking, over and over checking, that she had not dreamed it, that it had all truly happened; the snake, the horror, the sights, the sounds. The Unimaginable.

The sky blazed. The telegraph poles trooped like silent, stricken mourners, from the southern horizon, up to the station, through the yard and away across the northern wilderness, finding nothing to say. Even the windmill sails stood stock still. Some time soon, Comity knew that grief would overrun her from head to foot, like a colony of ants. For now, she seemed to be shrouded round in a fleecy weariness that made her stupid, vacant, clueless.

"But what of the piano, Mary?" That was what her father had said. What kind of words are those to say to someone dying? *But what of the piano, Mary?* What did it mean?

Skinny little Fred, the yard boy, came up behind her. For once she even heard him coming, because his hands were full of large round stones that rolled and grated against one another. He had painted them with dots of colour, matchstick figures, animals, patterns.

"Words," he said, pointing to a zigzag squiggle of paint. "Missus like words bigly." Dear, kind Fred.

Comity laid the stones round the head of the grave, so that the place would still show, even after some whipping wind had whirled the dirt around. She tried to ensure that the matchstick figures were well spaced out, patrolling the perimeter of the grave, keeping the ants at bay. Fred turned others over so that the "writing" was face-down where Mrs. Pinny might appreciate it.

Then they looked up and saw the thing coming.

Comity was more sure than ever that she was dreaming. An angular monster of immense size loomed over the ridge amid a plume of red dust, rolling and rocking as it came, warped by the wavy heat rising out of the ground. The shape gained four spindly legs, as the camel beneath it emerged into sight. A camel wearing a house: that was the impression.

As the beast came closer, they could see it was bearing not one but two vast slabs – one on each side of its hump: a wooden crate on one side, a metal tank of slopping water on the other. The tank was a counterweight: without it, presumably, the camel would simply keel over sideways into a tremendous noise of splintering wood. The outlandish shape lumbered towards them through a blizzard of flying things. The tank's stale water had drawn countless insects and birds. The camel had become a travelling oasis. A single crow perched supreme on the summit of the wooden crate, which was leaking music every jarring step of the way. Behind it came two more camels, lumpy with bundles and boxes.

One by one, various other people caught sight of the

camel train and came to stare. Camel trains came by once a month, but had never delivered anything like this before. Comity ran into the house. "Pa! Pa! Camels in the yard!"

Her father did not turn to face her. He was sitting in the machine room, hands clasped on the table edge. The short stems of hair that always stuck out above his ears quivered violently: she could see the Macassar oil hanging like teardrops from every strand.

"Camels in the yard, Pa. Load as big as a house!"

He did not move.

When Mary Triggers said yes to Herbert Pinny's offer of marriage, he'd had to ask her again: yes was not the answer he had been expecting. He knew he was nothing much to look at: a timid man with some absurd, finicky ways. Why would anyone – let alone Mary Triggers – agree to marry him?

Mary told him he would get used to the idea in time. But he never did.

Four years later, disastrously, he was promoted and awarded the post of Stationmaster at Kinkindele Telegraph Repeater Station Number Four.

The Overland Telegraph Line was two thousand miles long, and the messages that pulsed along its Wire could no more complete the journey non-stop than a man who set out to walk from coast to coast. Without refreshment they would fail and die on the journey. So at regular intervals along the Wire were "Repeater Stations" where telegraphers helped the flagging messages on their way. It was work of great importance…but it meant living in the loneliest, most godforsaken patches of nowhere on the whole continent of Australia.

But for love of Herbert, Mary left behind the sea, her well-to-do mother, her oh-so-respectable sister, her walnut-veneered Hapsburg Beale piano, libraries, concerts and civilization in general, to live at a tiny outpost of the British-Australian Telegraph Company, ninety miles from the nearest anywhere.

Her new life swarmed with insects. Snuffling, unseen animals spied on her from behind every bush. The laundry she hung on the clothes line turned red whenever the wind stirred up the dust. Her pet cat was gutted by an eagle hawk… But to Herbert's bewildered disbelief, Mary stayed on, reading aloud to him after dinner, teaching Comity her letters and numbers, teaching herself the Morse code so that "some day I might be almost as clever as you, dearest Herbert".

A deputy telegrapher arrived to share Herbert's workload – a handsome boy called Leonard, who naturally fell instantly in love with Mary Pinny. Jealous fear caused Herbert to lie awake each night clutching his aching chest, thinking he was going to die.

But amazingly Mary did *not* love Leonard back: not a bit! Leonard (being both heartbroken and sensible) wrote a letter of resignation, apologized for any inconvenience, and left with the very next camel train.

Herbert held the letter of resignation over the oil lamp and watched it burn. He found he did not want a deputy: better to manage on his own. (Mary could always help out, now that she had learned Morse.) Let Leonard's wages go on being paid into his bank: the Company need never know that Kinkindele had no deputy telegrapher.

And besides, the next one might not be as honourable as Leonard and might manage to snatch Mary's love away.

There were other men on the station, of course, but they did not worry Herbert so much. There was Smith the blacksmith – a man the same width in every direction. There was smelly Mr. Sankey the land manager, who ran the little farm which surrounded Telegraph House, and the Aboriginal stockmen who were so good with the goats and cows and sheep. Three wiremen lived over the barn – Amos, Hart and Cage – though they were gone for much of the time, checking and mending the Wire.

The precious Wire. That frail pencil line on the map

gave purpose to everyone who worked for the British-Australian Telegraph Company. It stretched across the entire continent, a wonder of the modern world, borne aloft by forty thousand poles. But he secretly knew of a greater miracle by far: Mary had chosen to live with him at Kinkindele Repeater Station. She could have won the love of the Company President himself, and yet she had chosen him. Even seven years on, he had not thought of a way of thanking her.

Then it came to him! He telegraphed his mother-in-law in Adelaide, and asked that Mary's piano be sent up by train and carrier. The shipping cost him two months' pay, but there could be no better use for money (especially in Kinkindele, where there was nothing to spend it on). When the piano arrived, Mary would be able to sit at it in the evenings and play Schubert and Schumann and Chopin. And the angels would gather overhead, jostling each other for the chance to hear pure joy plinking out of the walnut-veneered Hapsburg Beale piano.

Then, in the bottom of the wash basket, busily sucking moisture out of the washing...a tiger snake.

A pale, freckled arm plunged in among the sheets and shirts.

A cry in the yard.

By the time Herbert reached Mary, she was past speech. Her eyes looked into his so intently, so imploringly, that he forbad himself to blink. And all he found to say was, "But what of the piano, Mary?"

He loathed himself for all the things he had failed to say instead. *But what of the piano?* How puzzled Mary must have been, too: he had kept his plan a secret, wanting the piano to be a surprise.

And the tiger snake had up and surprised her first.

"Camels in the yard, Pa. Load as big as a house!" said his daughter's voice behind him. "I think it's a piano!"

Herbert swallowed down the bile in his throat. "Tell them no. It's too late. Tell them to take it back," he said.

When Comity went outside again, the camel with the piano had brought its load right up to the house. She stepped outdoors directly into its square shadow. The wooden crate towered over her head, blotting out the sun. Smith the smith came at a waddling run. Even the Aboriginal stockmen turned up (though as a rule they would not go anywhere near the Afghan camel-drivers).

The other camels watched with interest from beyond the gate.

No one seemed to have any idea how to offload the piano. It was Fred the yard boy who came up with the idea of dragging straw bales out of the barn and piling them up underneath the crate – to catch it as it came down.

"Pa says…"

The camel's head swung round at the sound of her voice, and Comity was enveloped in the stink of its breath. She could not help seeing how its ribs bulged downwards between its front legs, distorted by the tremendous weight it had lugged a hundred and more miles from the railway at Oodnadatta. Why did her father not come out? Why must she be the one to say it?

"Don't fetch it down. Pa says to take it back."

The tails of the camel-drivers' turbans were wound around their faces, covering all but their bloodshot eyes – eyes that did not rest on Comity even when she spoke. The cameleers were not accustomed to looking station females in the eye, let alone exchanging words with them.

"It came too late," said Comity. "You took too long. You have to take it back."

Wireman Amos explained to the camel-drivers about the Stationmaster's wife dying. The ghans did not understand – did not respond, anyway – and simply set about unstrapping the piano and water tank from either side of the camel's hump. Comity could not manage to say it more than three times over before her voice dwindled away to nothing.

The crate came down safely into the arms of seven men and a boy. The water tank fell with a thud, rolled over and nicked a slice out of the camel's belly, so that the animal moaned and stumbled backwards.

"Oh, you poor beast!" cried Comity involuntarily. The handsome ghan youth holding its lead-rope glanced at her, as if to say, *You were happy for her to carry it all the way back to Oodna.*

The spilled water from the tank soaked instantly into the ground, leaving only a gravel of drowned flies. The chickens rushed in to peck them up.

Then Amos, Cage and Hart broke open the crate and somehow wrestled the iron-framed piano up onto the verandah of Telegraph House. But when Smith tried the front door, it would not open.

The piano's candleholders slipped round to point at the floor, like a thumbs-down.

The men looked sullen: Mr. Pinny ought at least to show his face, even if he was built too puny to lend a hand with the lifting. Fred, who had never seen a piano in his life, lifted the lid and, seeing the keys, mistook them for teeth and dropped it again, loudly and heavily. Smith slapped him round the head.

Comity tried to think what her mother would do. "Thank you, gentlemen," she said clearly and politely. "I expect you would care for some refreshment before you go about your business."

Everyone cheered up. Comity pushed at the door of Telegraph House herself. Still it did not open. With her hand on the doorknob, she could feel it softly vibrating, and realized that her father was leaning against the other side of the door, holding it shut. "I shall bring you out lemonade, gentlemen," said Comity. "In a moment."

Fred smiled encouragingly. The camel shook itself, easing its bones back into place with a noise like an ancient leather couch creaking. It dropped a mountain of dung, then broke away to amble around the yard, trample a flower bed and get its neck caught in the washing line. Laundry that Mary Pinny had hung up but not lived to take down again capsized onto the hard-packed red earth. Shirts and sheets tangled around the camel's feet.

Then it came.

Like a dust storm, grief spun in through the myrtle trees and smashed Comity in the face, choking, stinging, blinding. She stood on the verandah and wailed and screamed and sobbed for the loss of her mother.

Smith, the wiremen, the Afghan cameleers and the stockmen disappeared as quickly as water soaks into dry ground.

CHAPTER TWO

Jesus' Gunyah

Herbert Pinny did not cry. He worked. He had always loved his job, prided himself on his skill and accuracy. Decoding and recoding Morse takes great concentration, assembling sentences out of the dots and dashes, clicks and silences. Now he found that it took his mind down a deep dark corridor to a small, soundproof room where nothing could reach him, not even the grief beating on the door, trying to get in.

He stayed in the machine room all day and sometimes all night too, because it was not safe to sleep. While a man sleeps, his enemies can creep up on him, pour dreams in at his ear and fill up his head with faces, fantasies, false

18

hopes. Coiled tiger snakes wait under a man's pillow, ready to whisper in his ear: *It is still true. She is still dead.*

He found he had to avoid Comity somewhat. A child's tears are as infectious as chickenpox. But the girl would cope. She was eleven after all – almost eleven – would be eleven soon. Children are resilient, and what good was he to her anyway: this father who had brought her to the middle of nowhere and so killed her mother? …No, no, hush! Concentrate, man, concentrate. Shut out everything but work.

So Herbert Pinny worked. He did not cry – which baffled and bewildered Comity. Some days she seemed to be drowning in tears. She thought she was signalling frantically for rescue, taking her father tea, touching his sleeve, trying to catch his eye. But Pinny only bent his head lower over his notebook.

No one else on the station wept either.

Was it wrong, then, to cry? Comity wondered. Was she supposed to be glad, because her mother was with Jesus in Heaven? No one else on the station seemed to be mourning – just avoiding her, extra-busily going about their work. Only her friend Fred, as he fed the chickens, sprinkled a few crumbs of comfort in her direction too.

"Trees cry also," he said, as Comity struggled to find a dry corner of handkerchief so as to blow her nose.

"Who do?"

So he took her to see the yarran trees and the red drops of gum welling out of their bark. "They been cry since Death get going," said Fred. "Beginning of the world, Maker Byamee hang up a bee nest in this tree – say to Begin Man and Begin Wife, *My world is your world now. Take what you want, no matter. Go all over where you want. But hands off this tree, you hear me?* One day the wife she picking up woodbits under yarran tree and she see honey-shine and she take one lick and she go at that tree lick-spit quite contrary to all what Byamee say. Wo-ho! Old Bat live in this tree. She shake up Old Bat and away he fly. Death Bat. He taking death all over everywhere. Sorry business for Begin Man and Begin Woman. Bat make big damn black shadow, him. Fly over me some day. Fly over you. Down go us. Tree so sad that tears run down still, yah?"

Comity sometimes wondered why Fred, who was younger (probably) than she was, knew more stories than she did. Maybe Aboriginals were born knowing stories, she speculated. Fred knew a limitless supply: stories oozed out of him, like gum from a yarran.

She looked closer at the red droplets, touched one with a finger. The gum was hard, not wet, and yet it was a comfort. It was. Just to know that someone other than she had openly cried. When she got back to the house she would tell Mama the story…

And there it was again, that electric jolt that shook her heart in its socket and made her want to spew up a gallon of tears.

"You ask Jesus?" said Fred.

"'Bout what? Creeping into His bosom for comfort?"

"Nah. Send the Missus back a while."

"Mama?!"

"He done it hisself. Come back."

"That was different. He had to make sure the Apostles had got things straight. Jesus never fetched anyone *else* back."

"Damn did."

"Damn did not."

"Damn did. Fellah Lazarus."

"Oh, him. Yes but he was family. Or a family friend, leastways."

"Jesus come round here pretty a lot. Missus call him friend." Fred was certain of this – Mrs. Pinny had sung it often enough: "What a friend we have in Jesus". He had particular cause to remember, because Mrs. Pinny had tried to teach him to sing it, and hymn singing had turned out to be nothing like Kinkindele native singing. It was a battle neither side had won.

*

Mary Pinny had not set out to teach Fred anything. Most of Comity's lessons took place on the verandah, though, and Fred had a way of finding himself a job to do nearby. One day, Comity looked down and saw, through a knothole in the wooden decking, the glimmer of a brown eye. She said nothing, not wanting to get Fred into trouble. But a week or two later, when the termites had been busy, Comity's chair leg went through the boards and narrowly missed skewering Fred in the head.

Comity's mother was not annoyed (except about the termites). She even asked if Fred would care to join the class. Of course, he refused point-blank. Somehow, though, the open-air classroom *expanded* to incorporate Fred. He came chiefly for the stories, and once Fred heard a story he never forgot it. Hence his extensive knowledge of the Bible and his certainty that Jesus and the Missus had been close friends. After all, stranger people than Jesus had moved into the Kinkindele district with the coming of the Wire. And any friend of the Missus was all right by Fred.

Secretly, Comity and the yarran trees were not the only ones to have shed tears over the dusty mound in the yard. Mary Pinny had smiled at Fred, included him, shared her stories with him, and in return he had adored her.

"How would I do it?" said Comity suddenly as they walked back from the yarran trees.

"What do?"

"Ask Jesus to send Mama back."

"Go in his gunyah. Ask him," said Fred with a shrug that suggested nothing could be easier. And of course there was only one place Jesus was likely to pitch camp at Kinkindele, and that was the paper store.

There was no actual chapel on the compound, but naturally Sundays could not go by without some kind of religious service. Sooner than open up Telegraph House to all and sundry, Pinny appointed the paper store as the station's place-of-worship. It was no bigger than a potting shed, but every Sunday, seven adults and a child would crowd inside, stand in a circle, elbow-to-elbow, recite a prayer, sing a hymn and listen to Pinny reading from the Bible. He read badly, leaving a space between words as if dictating a telegraph. And Comity, standing opposite him, could see his forefinger knocking out the Morse against the seam of his trouser leg. Sometimes he even punctuated out of sheer habit. "*A man went down to Jericho stop.*" "*Jesus wept stop.*" To her shame, Comity found herself wishing her mother would take over; she read so b-e-a-yutifully and made everything come real.

Smith would not have Fred inside the chapel, but made

him stand outside and listen. (Comity quite thought it was because the store was too small for eight. She did not realize she was supposed to look down on the Aboriginals: her mother and father never had.) Shut out of Jesus' gunyah, Fred imagined the place to contain powerful spiritual magic. If he had been allowed inside, he would have found nothing very awe-inspiring about the stacks of forms, shelves of spare parts, or the smell of Smith's armpits. Comity tried explaining to Fred that Jesus did not actually *live* in the stationery store, but when Fred got hold of a wrong idea he gripped it so tight that it was hard for anyone to remember he was wrong.

By the time they got back from the weeping yarran trees, Comity's own tears had dried to salt stripes on her cheeks and her heart was straining free of despair. She *would* ask Jesus to bring her mother back from the dead!

The paper store was kept locked, because, as well as paper, it contained kerosene, battery acid, methylated spirits and solder, sheep drench and some valuable coils of fine wire. The Company was fearful of thieving natives. Head Office was fond of warning the stations against "thieving natives". (Head Office – like Fred – could be very convincing once they got an idea into their heads.) Comity fetched the key from the house and unlocked the door, as she had done countless times before. Now, though, her hands were shaking uncontrollably and her mouth was dry at the thought of an interview with Jesus.

She would not ask forever. Just long enough for Mama to see her piano and maybe teach Comity to play a tune on it. Just for long enough to get her mother's face and hands and hair fixed in her mind so she would never forget them…oh, and to tell her about seeing that flock of budgerigars – and about the yarran trees crying. Just for long enough to say sorry for cracking open Pilgrim's Progress *that time, so that the pages fell out, and for putting it back on the shelf and not owning up. And just for long enough to make Father go outdoors sometimes and go to bed once in a while.*

"Will you come in with me?" said Comity, and Fred was there like a shot. For years he had been aching to see inside Jesus' gunyah. Besides, he too wanted Mrs. Pinny back.

Inside, Comity propped up *The Light of the World* picture that was forever falling off the wall. With Jesus there in the painting, knocking at that door, holding up his lantern, the stationery store already felt lighter.

"I don't have my Sunday bonnet on!" she whispered suddenly, aghast. "A lady cannot just wear hair in church!"

So Fred wound her hair up on top of her head, like a lardy cake, and stuck a pencil through the knot of sun-blonded strands. Then they kneeled on the floor, shoulder to shoulder, and prayed for Jesus to think again about taking Mrs. Pinny to his bosom, and to raise her back to life as He had with his pal Lazarus.

"Or Jairus! You raise up that Jairus gal also!" put in Fred, in case Jesus had forgotten.

As the sun moved over Telegraph House and shone on the outhouse, pecked lines of sunlight showed through gaps in the plank walls, as if Comity and Fred were in a golden cage whose frame was glowing hot. Sweat trickled down the nape of Comity's neck. *"Give her back, sir! Please! We cannot do without her, nor anyone can!"*

Then the door flew open and Smith grabbed Fred by the hair and threw him outside to land on his back amid the chickens. The blacksmith picked him up and threw him down again several times, then set about methodically kicking him.

"What you doing, Mr. Smith? Stop! Mr. Smith, stop!" yelled Comity, dragging on the man's shirt: her two hands could not circle the great thickness of his wrist.

Smith took off his belt, vowing on his mother's life to beat the very flesh off Fred's bones. Perhaps he meant to go for his trouser belt. If he deliberately chose the broader band of saddle leather buckled round his loins, he was forgetting why he wore it: to relieve a double hernia and a back strain. His back twinged; his hernias swelled, and he was obliged to give up. Fred bolted under the pole fence.

Infected by the violence in the air, the chickens pecked out each others' head feathers.

Smith ran limpingly over to Telegraph House and Comity trotted after him, baffled as to what crime Smith thought had been committed. What did he have against praying? Even as she squeezed past the piano on the verandah, she could hear Smith's ranting, clear through the house wall:

"*...can't be trusted...not fit company...no daughter of mine would be...*" His voice, harsh as a saw rasping through wood, snagged on knotholes of pain as he clutched at his back or belly.

Herbert Pinny was not accustomed to stationhands barging into the house. Startled to his feet, he had knocked over his stool. He looked panicked rather than outraged. "What were you and the boy doing in the stationery store, Comity?"

"Praying to Jesus, Papa! Fred and I were praying to Jesus about Mama!"

Her father peered at her like a man trying to wake out of a deep sleep. He looked for all the world as if he had more important things to think about than Jesus or resurrection.

"Now I heard everything," fumed Smith. "*His kind? Praying?*"

"Mr. Smith kicked Fred, Papa!"

"Fred acted contrary to Regulations," said her father. "He should not have entered the store. Unauthorized persons are not permitted on Company property."

"Kicked him three times, Papa!" said Comity.

"Regulations..." said Herbert Pinny.

"*He touched her hair!*" blared Smith and dared Comity to deny it.

She pulled the pencil out of her topknot. She wanted very much to ram its point into Smith's hernias, but instead she explained – very slowly, very fully – about the store being the chapel, and about not having her Sunday bonnet and about Fred fixing up her hair.

Forced to back down, Smith began rebuckling his broad belt. He assured Mr. Pinny that he had never – no, never for a moment! – suspected Miss Comity of any misconduct; only the blackfellah. Comity was bewildered. What kind of misconduct was ever done in a paper store, let alone a chapel?

"Praying indeed. Thieving, more like. Check the stock: that's what you need to do now, sir." Smith added this new excuse for kicking Fred.

Herbert Pinny moved some forms about on the countertop. "I..." Regulations, it was true, did require him to keep a close check on Telegraph Company property.

If there was a chance Fred had pilfered from the store, Pinny ought to investigate it. Unhappily, he followed Smith to the sunlit doorway before coming to a halt. (Comity half expected him to stretch out a hand and check for rain.) He bent and refastened the laces of one shoe. He did up a waistcoat button that had come undone. Finally, he stepped out onto the verandah. The sight of the piano made him flinch.

Spring was written, in an elegant calligraphy of white clouds, across an azure sky. A never-settling snow of thistledown danced and hovered in the air. A pair of wallabies seemed to be comparing their front paws, over by the fence. Black cockatoos were sitting in the myrtle trees.

Smith set off for the paper store and Comity followed at a run (in case he took something, just to make Fred look guilty). When they looked back, the Stationmaster was skirting the yard, keeping close to the buildings. Where there were no buildings, he clung to the pole fence instead, eyes screwed almost shut against the sunlight. He looked for all the world as if he was afraid of the open air. With a last clumsy burst of speed, he crossed the threshold of the stationery store to find the other two staring at him, and turned his face away.

Watched by *The Light of the World*, he checked all the shelves in the store, blank-eyed. "There is nothing amiss here." Finding Comity's Bible, he opened it, and was ambushed by his wife's handwriting on the flyleaf:

*To our darling daughter Comity
on her birthday…*

He threw it back onto the shelf as if it had burned him.

"Lock up and replace the key on the keyboard please, Comity," he said, and found his way back to Telegraph House around the perimeter of the yard, like a blind man feeling his way.

"Did Smith hurt you?" Comity asked Fred when she found him in among the blue gum trees.

"That *goona*?" He snorted his contempt. She sat down beside him. "One day I go Altjeringa," he said. "Fetch back *my* mama too."

"Where's that? Far off?"

"Altjeringa. Land of Maker Byamee. I say, 'Give her back, Byamee *kubang*. Big mistake you make taking her. She formidable bad cook. One day she poison you like-as-not. You send her back to me, you should. Let her poison me." He ran the heel of one hand across his cheekbone.

"Your ma's dead too? I never knew!" Comity was shocked. How was it you could know someone for ages and yet not know major things about them?

"Long time."

"I'm sorry. I always thought the laundry lady Lulu was your ma." This seemed both to astonish and insult Fred, so she added hastily, "Your dead people go to Altjeringa and live with Maker Byamee, do they?"

"Yay."

When Comity asked how Fred would get up into the sky in order to meet the creator god, he corrected her geography. He knew the journey was overland because once, in Dreamtime, a hero called Yooneerara had walked there for a look, without waiting to be dead. "Byamee bigly pleased with him: *That some walk, kurlang! You my kind of man!*"

The story of Yooneerara was long – Comity's attention drifted sometimes, but it was restful to hear Fred yamble on. His vocabulary was full of words he had learned from Mrs. Pinny and Sunday service; somehow that made his stories all the more soothing.

"Can I come?" she interrupted before he had even finished. "When you go to Altjeringa, can I come?"

"Yay, Lilly-Pilly. Jesus be there also maybe I bet. What a friend Byamee have in Jesus."

But Comity's admiration for Jesus had taken rather a downturn. She had been thinking. Apart from the nastiness in the stationery store (which He could easily have prevented), there was the matter of the tiger snake. How hard would it have been for Jesus to stretch out a finger and kill the snake in the wash basket? And yet He had done nothing. He could have expunged all tiger snakes from the entire world. But no, He had just stood by with his lantern, His fresh-washed robe, that smug look on His face, and let the snake kill Mama and slither away, scot-free. He had just stood there, knocking on a door, thinking about nothing except wanting to get indoors and stay there and not come out again.

CHAPTER THREE

Breaking the News

Herbert Pinny did not reach out a finger either, except to tap his Morse key.

He received messages, decoded them onto his notepad, then recoded and sent them on, his finger on the Morse key, tap-tap-tapping until the used page of the notepad could be torn off and impaled on a metal spike.

```
COME HOME FATHER AILING


1000 MERINO READY


DELAYED STOP DO NOT WAIT SHEARING
```

ARRIVE DARWIN TUESDAY FORENOON

SOLICITOR WANTS PROOF OF DEATH

Other people's lives, other people's worries, other people's business; other people's joys and tragedies. All of them came into Herbert Pinny's machine room, briefly rattled at his eardrums, then passed through his hands and on across the awful, unimaginable distance to the other side of the continent. The words came, the words went, but Herbert Pinny stayed, impaled on the sharp metal spike of duty, at one lonely spot on the map.

Comity worried about him, worried how little he ate and how few recipes she knew. She worried whether the piano waiting patiently on the verandah would make him sadder indoors or out. She worried whether he had ordered more supplies, whether he ever slept. Her father told her he had asked Head Office for a new telegrapher, and a governess to continue Comity's education, but she had no idea how long they would take to pack their cabin trunks and make the journey up from Adelaide.

She took to fastening up her hair with a pencil that way Fred had done it, because "up" was more grown up. And she did so need to be grown up.

The first time he saw her hair like this, Herbert Pinny

uttered a cry and dropped a forkful of beans, reminded of his wife. The stationhands, too, looked strangely at her fastened-up hair and said how she would make someone "a proper little wife one day", then glanced at each other. Cage turned chivalrous and offered to get the piano into Telegraph House.

So, finally it came indoors, making about as much noise as an ox sliding down a mountainside in a tin bath. But once it was in the living room, Comity did not dare touch its keys or attempt to pick out a tune, for fear of upsetting her father. She covered it in a sheet and they both did their best to ignore it.

At night, Comity lay in bed trying to decode the erratic beating of her heart. (She knew Morse, of course: her mother had taught it to her, along with the alphabet, ironing and simple fractions.) Sometimes Comity was sure she could make out letters – an H or an F or an S – and wondered if her mother was somehow signalling her from Heaven. She began to listen for an L, an O, a V, an E.

"When will the new man be coming, Papa?" she asked one night, about six weeks after the funeral.

He did not answer, scratching anxiously at a spot of

grease on his trouser leg. When she offered to fetch a damp cloth, he only reached into his waistcoat pocket and pulled out a pellet of paper.

"A message came in today from your grandmother," he said and unfolded the pellet, smoothing it, over and over and over, with the pepper pot, until it split down the creases. Comity went and picked it up before it was shredded past reading.

```
MARY
RECEIVED NO BIRTHDAY GREETING STOP
HOPE ALL IS WELL STOP DID PIANO ARRIVE
MOTHER
```

Comity could almost smell the hurt feelings rising off the paper. On her sixtieth birthday, Grandma Triggers had not heard from her youngest daughter.

"You did not tell Grandma?"

Her father ran his tongue round his mouth as if looking for words lodged between his back teeth, but came up with no excuse. "You may write her a letter informing her."

"Me?"

"A small enough kindness to do your grandmother, surely?" he said, returning to the stain on his trouser leg.

"But could you not...?" Comity began.

Her father folded his napkin six times, then went back to the machine room, leaving the supper on his plate, cold but not untouched. Each bean had been separated from every other, using the tines of his fork, so that each stood isolated in a desert of white china.

Comity sat down to write the letter telling her grandmother that her daughter Mary was dead.

Dear Grandmamma
Happy birthday. We would have comunicatied before
but were too sad

Dear Grandmother,
I hope you passed a pleasing birthday. Many
apollogies for the lateness of this letter. Mother
might have written but she

Dear Grandmother Triggers
Mama did not write becuase she is ~~dead~~ I
thought Father wrote. I think Father did not write
because he did not want to make you sad. Nor me.

Dear Grandmother
It is with great sorrow that we write to inform
you that Mary Pinny your daughter passed away

37

to a better place on account of a tiger snake in
the wash basket and it happened before your
birthday.

Comity sharpened the pencil and started again:

Dear Mama,
I am sorry I missed your birthday. The Wire was
down and the camel train did not come by. I hope
you had a grand day. Sixty? It cannot be! I bet
you are as beayutiful as ever you was.
    How are the cats? How is the nitting coming
along? I am nitting a saddlecloth for dear Comity.
Did I tell you she now has a snow-white pony with
a star on his nose? She rides very well. Without
stirrups even. The ponies name is Ivanhoe like in
Ivanhoe which I was reading to Comity when ~~xxxx~~
    The garden is looking a verittable paradise
with a fountain and fish pool. Of a Sunday after
church we take a picnic out there and eat
mangroves.
    Mr Smith has a hurnia front and back, but
I am sure he deserves it. I am very very well,
but the washing line fell down in a heap which was
a sore bother.

The piano came sound and safe on a camel with a big tank of water. Thank you thank you. Now I play each sunset. Motzart and those others. When we visit you one day we will make a birthday consert for you, dear Mamma.

When the letter was done, Comity found she had leaned so hard on the pencil that readable words were gouged in the tabletop: *pony dear well*. Her jaw was stiff, her eyeballs dry, her finger dented from gripping the pencil so tightly. Comity twisted her hair upwards and refastened it with the pencil. For a few moments all had been well again. For a few minutes she had conjured up her mother, and her b-e-a-yutiful mother had (of course) thought up much better, happier things to say. Grandma Triggers need not be upset. Nobody need be upset.

It was ridiculous, of course. The handwriting was nothing like Mary Pinny's. The spelling was sure to be wrong here and there: not all the spelling rules were as easy to remember as b-e-a-yutiful.

The very next time her father went to the outside toilet, Comity crept into the machine room to send a telegram to her grandmother telling her the truth:

FONDEST BIRTHDAY WISHES BUT SAD NEWS TOO BAD FOR WORDS

The necessary dots and dashes swarmed like ants through her head. The Morse key was smooth and pleasant to touch...

"*What are you doing, child?*" Before she had tapped out one word, her father was standing behind her in the doorway.

"You wanted me to—"

"Were you meddling with the machine? You know never to touch the machine. Company Regulations..."

"I know, I know."

"Must I lock the door to the machine room every time I visit the dunny? I think I should be able to trust my own daughter!"

"Of course you can, Papa. ...Would you like some berries mashed up in milk?"

And then there was no time for second thoughts. The next day was Sunday, but Herbert Pinny did not turn up for Sunday service in the stationery store. They waited ten minutes for him, and Comity felt oddly irritated. She had been happy sitting in among the myrtle trees, feeding imaginary carrots to her imaginary pony Ivanhoe. She was angered, too, by the looks the men exchanged with each other; by the way her Sunday bonnet would not fit over her topknot; by the fact that Fred was not allowed to come in. *The Light of the World* still wore that smug look on His face. She picked up the Bible and read aloud from boring Leviticus. Serve them all right.

As soon as Sunday service was over, she tore open the letter to Grandma Triggers and added a postscript.

PS I spoke this letter out loud and Comity wrote it down. You most likely gessed this. I berned my fingers a little cooking and it pains me to write.

Even as she signed her mother's name, a cry went up outside of "Camels a-coming!" – a cry that invariably set her heart bouncing. Living on a station as remote as Kinkindele, the sight of outsiders brought wondrous possibilities…and also a kind of fear.

Comity shook herself. What was she thinking of? This camel train would surely be bringing the replacement telegrapher! Quickly, she made lemonade, checked her hair in the speckled mirror by the door, and went out to greet the newcomer. *"I prepared your bed, Mr. X,"* she practised saying. *"If there is anything you require…"*

The big barrel-chests of the camels bulged over the rail fence. The ghans turned their faces away the moment she appeared. Comity would have loved to avert her eyes too, but she needed to spot the new telegrapher and say all the polite things she had thought up.

But there was no telegrapher.

There were only the ghans and their camels, and the flies that came with the camels, and the bales of cable, the hoof-trimmer, the porcelain insulators, banana saplings sent to Mary Pinny by nice Mr. Boyce at Repeater Station Three. There was a book in torn wrappings, which Mary Pinny had requested from the bookseller in Oodna. There was the usual fat envelope from Comity's Aunt Berenice.

But there was no telegrapher.

Another month to wait. Another month of coping.

Rise above it, her mother had always said. *That's why angels were given wings – to rise above life's trials.*

She took the official papers indoors to her father. He had not so much as left his stool. He had not so much as stood up to greet his new assistant. He sat bent-backed over the desk, wearing his dapper black suit, the blinds lowered, the clock muffled up, to silence its tick. The fat yellow cable from the Morse machine coiled between his knees and emerged from under the stool. From behind, he looked for all the world like a giant rat, nibbling.

"So…did you *not* send for a new assistant, Papa?"

The giant rat swung round on its stool and attempted a smile. "We are well enough on our own, are we not,

Comity? I think Kinkindele is able to manage without the cost of a second telegrapher." His eyelids were red and rheumy. In rubbing them to stay awake, he had rubbed machine oil into his eyes, along with several eyelashes, and the whites had become inflamed. He looked almost as if he was weeping red gum.

"Of course we can, Papa," said Comity.

She did not trouble to ask about the governess. After all, who ever wanted one of those in place of a mother?

CHAPTER FOUR

Fibs, Lies and Other Stories

The letter to her grandmother weighed on Comity's conscience. Lying was a terrible crime, she knew – one that would have made her mother angry. *"Comity, I am as cross as the Scottish flag!"*

Comity did just remember her grandmother, but only as someone unapproachable, associated with itch. The unapproachable-ness came of the knitting needles forever waggling in Grandma's hands. The itch came of the knitted garments she made for Comity. The clearest memory she had was of Grandma Triggers sitting very erect, strands of different colour wool stretching out in every direction – a grey spider-woman at the centre of a brilliant web.

Wearing Grandma Triggers's knitting had given Comity a lifelong sympathy for sheep, who had to go about always in woollen garments and could not even take them off when no one was looking. Grandma's letters were filled with news of the things she was making. Even her handwriting looked as if it had been knitted in two-ply green ink. Adventure did not feature anywhere.

The Triggers family had moved to Australia from Scotland. Adventures *might* have happened there. Perhaps Grandpa Triggers had been exciting before he died.

"What did Grandpa Triggers do?" she asked. But her father had stopped answering questions.

By contrast, Fred's ancestors were unforgettable. Fred's best ancestor had kept six smooth stones in his dillybag, and when he took them out and rubbed them in lizard fat they turned into sons who went out hunting for him and, while they were about it, taught everyone how to use throwing sticks and have babies. Fred himself carried six stones in his dillybag, probably to honour his ancestor. But then Fred carried a shrivelled-up dead bandicoot baby in his dillybag too, and he said that was "just in case".

Comity took to carrying a pair of knitting needles around with her, to honour her ancestors. But never wool.

To hear Fred talk, you'd think all of his ancestors were still alive.

And he knew about so many monsters and oddities! There were the mischievous Tuckonies, who played tricks on people; the min-min lights, which followed a person about. There were the Dhinnabarrada, who could turn you into an emu just by touching you; the Kadimakara, big as a house, which fell through a hole in the sky and couldn't get back so had to get by on eating people; and the Devil-Devil, who ripped people limb from limb given half a chance… Fred talked about them as if they did not scare him *at all*. The only monsters Comity knew personally were the thorny devils (which only ate ants really) and the hideous spiders who hung themselves up in the barn. Tiger snakes, of course.

And her cousins in Adelaide. The noxious Blighs.

The camel train had brought a letter from them – the usual long letter from Aunt Berenice, praising her three marvellous children. In the past, there had been huge fun to be got from these letters, because Mother had read them out loud, imitating her sister's snobby voice.

"*Last week Alexander was declared quite the best in his dance class… Papa entertained us last evening on the flute, while Anne accompanied him on the piano to delightful effect…*"

In fact Mary Pinny invented "Bligh letters" just to make them laugh at dinner time. "*Alexander has learned to fly.*

Papa hollowed out his potato last evening at dinner and played the Hallelujah Chorus on it, while Anne improvised a harmony on the aspidistra. Dear little Albert…"

When, through his laughter, Herbert suggested she was not being very sisterly, she retorted, "What? These are the people who sent us wine glasses for a wedding present, knowing full well that we do not drink! *Huh* to sisterly!"

What unwitting joy Aunt Berenice had given with her braggarty letters. Now, the latest travel-stained envelope was nothing but a wedge of heartache. Comity tore it open. No need to ask whether her father had telegraphed news to them of Mary's death. He had not, or Aunt Berenice would have used a black-bordered envelope.

"Would you be good enough, Comity, to write informing Aunt Berenice…"

"Yes, father. Of course I will."

"It occurs to me…" He looked at her out of the corner of his eyes. "Aunt Berenice might offer you a home with her, so that you may attend school in Adelaide and complete your education."

A surge of angry dismay went through Comity. Send her to live with Aunt Berenice? Was this the man who had said he and Comity could manage to run the station between them? And was he ready to pack her off to Adelaide to live with the noxious Blighs? Let him do without a deputy telegrapher or a governess to break his precious concentration. If he thought he could do without Comity too, then he could think again!

Rise above it, kitten, said her mother's voice inside her head.

Rise above it as the angels do

said her mother's embroidery on the wall. Comity took the newly delivered book, in its torn wrappers, and ran outside to the myrtle bushes.

But when she opened the parcel, the ants had got there ahead of her. The pages had been eaten into a lacework of holes.

"What you doing?" Fred asked when he found her there, rocking to and fro, eyes shut, lips clamped between her teeth.

"Rising above it," said Comity.

Fred was no end impressed. "How high you get up?"

It was too hard to explain, and Comity knew she could not get through telling him without crying, which would not be rising above anything. So she offered to read him a story from the book, which was a sure way of silencing him.

The ribbony sentences had been chopped into bits by the insects. Whole paragraphs yawned with crevasses. Dead ants peppered what was left with extra punctuation.

But Comity rose above all that. Out of a title, a few nouns and some chewed verbs, she assembled a sort of story. So shutting her eyes, she invented the adventures of a poor lace-maker ordered to make dresses for twelve spoiled kangaroo princesses using only the wings of moths, the honey-bags of ants and a bucket of snow from the grate of Balmoral Castle at the other end of the world.

Just as the Wularu of Balmoral pounced, a sharpness dug into Comity's shoulder and, with a squeal, she found Fred's pointy chin resting there. Hoping the gift of reading might have come to him magically overnight, he was looking to see if the lace-maker was going to survive.

"You awake-dreaming!" he said delightedly. "Good as any blackfellah, you awake-dreaming! I do this also! Utterly the brain go out your head and run about all over!"

"Sometimes I do make things up," she confessed.

But Fred's face was full of admiration. "Like your ma. You a stout chap with a yamble! You the whole best person round this goonawodli."

Not since the funeral had anyone praised Comity for anything. Kindness is very undermining. Just when you think you have risen above the tribulations sent to test you, there you are, weeping like a yarran tree.

"Pa wants to send me away to the noxious Blighs in Adelaide and I hate them and I hate him and I am meant to love everyone but he does not love anybody at all so why do I have to?"

Fred turned a leisurely backward somersault.

"Is curlew-cursed, the bossman," he said, as matter-of-fact as a doctor diagnosing measles.

And he told her the story of Mopoke the Owl hiding in a cave and Curlew-bird jeering and sneering at him from outside, cursing him never to come out, never to see daylight again or be friends with another living creature.

"Consequinkly, Mopoke he cry all night along – *Hoo booo, hoo booo* all night along. You listen."

Comity's parched heart drank up every word. First she felt pity for poor Mopoke, and then the feeling spilled over and she was able to feel it for her father too, cursed with a dread of the outdoors, of open doors, of letting anyone in.

"You mean Pa can't help it?"

What a relief to feel pity! What a relief to understand her father again!

Comity resolved that she was not going *anywhere*, and thanks to the paper-eating ants, she knew exactly how to stay put. It would not be selfish or wicked. Her father was curlew-cursed and had to be looked after; her mother would have been the first to agree. And it was *such* a relief.

"You are my very best friend, Fred," said Comity.

"You got more?" said Fred.

"Plenty." Comity laughed, and felt the warm breath on her neck of Ivanhoe her imaginary snow-white pony.

CHAPTER FIVE

Making it Up

Dear Cousins,

How are you? Are you well? We send three cheers for your good news. We have a fine orkestra now ourselfs, what with Loud Lulu on the bagpipes and Amos playing his bugel and Cage the violin. Father plays glass harmonica on the crystal wine glasses. Naturally we do not use them for <u>drinking wine, because we do not drink wine and never have.</u>

Emus are roosting on the roof today. In Denmark this brings luck and Papa says we need a lot of luck so we need a lot of emus.

Mama is v bizzy at present helping

Comity stopped short in the nick of time. She had been going to write that her mother was helping out in the Morse room, but that was a lie which could have got Herbert Pinny dismissed from his job. Comity knew full well that Unauthorized Persons using the machine room was forbidden. What was more, the noxious Blighs knew it too: Mr. Bligh was Superintendent of Telegraphy.

Mama is v bizzy at present helping to sheer the sheep. She is a wonder with a pare of sheers.

Aunt Berenice was *never* going to offer Comity a home, because Aunt Berenice would never, never, never, ever know that her sister was dead. Comity vowed to make sure of that.

Forbidden to help in the machine room, bereft of lessons, Comity spent more and more time with Fred. When Amos, Hart and Cage left for a northerly tour of inspection, Smith the smith took to "resting his back" in the afternoons. This involved lying on the bench in the forge and doing deep breathing and inspecting the inside of his eyelids until sunset. He knew full well that the Stationmaster would not check up on him. The Stationmaster never stepped outside the house.

Meanwhile, Comity and Fred explored the surrounding countryside together, venturing farther and farther from the station. Fred knew every inch of the landscape. Comity firmly believed that he knew every inch of Australia.

He took Comity to see the cat tree, where dead feral cats and dingoes had been strung up to frighten off live ones. (It gave her nightmares for a week.) He pointed out the widow-maker trees that would drop their branches on anyone stupid enough to sleep in their shade. He took her to places that were beautiful and mysterious and strange, where the bones of rock poked through the earth's downy skin or the sinking sun made eagles out of the evening cloud. He pointed out where native corroborees had lasted all night, and what stories had been told there, and what dancing and magic done.

He knew of rocks that had been Old People during the Dreamtime. Growing weary, they had simply hunkered down and turned to stone. The spirits of men and women came out of such rocks – "Never when you do looking, but when you do not looking, they come forth." And Comity began to see the Outback as Fred saw it, full of wonder and beauty and stories.

Fred, too, was learning. His English was improving. In their dealings with the station, most of the Aboriginals spoke very little. But Fred had not only found a friend in Comity, he had found an audience for his cleverness. If he could, Fred would have kept Comity in his dillybag along with the bandicoot and the six stones (and the reel of fuse wire he had indeed stolen from Jesus' gunyah).

So he was even ready to show her his greatest secret of all – the carcass of a railway carriage lying on its side in a hollow near Deep Brook. It had the desired effect.

"Oh Fred! However did it get here?"

"It crash," he said. "There was big crash-bang nearby Oodna. A camel, maybe. Ask not why the wild camel joys to walk on rail track. They do it."

Some passing ghans had helped to free the dead and injured, then, by way of a reward, they had taken the only carriage still upright after the crash. For a time, it had rolled along pretty well behind four camels harnessed to it by ropes. But in reaching Miser's Gorge, the ghans had not known how to apply the brakes, and the carriage had rolled down the slope, crushing two of the camels before rolling onto its side. It lay there now, abandoned. The remains of the dead camels were still in evidence, inside and outside the carriage, bones stripped bare by dingoes, crows and insects and bleached by the blazing sun.

Though he worked at Kinkindele Station and slept nearby with the other stationhands, Fred thought of the railway carriage as his true gunyah. Until today, he had shown it to no one. He climbed up onto it now, opened one of the doors, and they both lowered themselves into the sweltering heat of a first class railcar.

Everything was askew, though Fred had cleared away any broken glass. A dented kettle rested on the side of the stove instead of the top. But with no water to be had, that was as good a place as any, Comity supposed.

"I make a brew-up?" asked Fred, and they made pretend tea and drank it.

There was even a suitcase and umbrella in the luggage rack, their owner dead or otherwise past caring about his property. Fred opened the suitcase now and put on a stiff collar, a pair of reading glasses and a stethoscope. He sucked on an unlit, empty pipe. Even without tobacco, it made the exact same noise as when Cage the wireman did it. Comity would have laughed, but something told her not to. Fred was investing himself with more than clothing when he put on collar and spectacles: the expression on his face changed; the set of his body altered.

"Will the ghans come back for it ever?" she asked.

Fred made a snarling noise in the back of his throat, as if to say he could defend his home if he had to.

"A person could live here," Comity said.

"A while," said Fred.

Fred's spur-of-the-moment decision to show Comity the railcar made them late in getting back to the station. Later than late.

Smith was up and raging. Cage, Hart and Amos had arrived home from their tour of inspection and two of their horses were in need of shoeing. Unable to find Fred to pump the forge bellows, Smith was instantly furious. When boy and girl appeared from between the blue gum trees, he snatched up a bridle by its reins and swung it round his head, swearing to slash Fred into jerky.

Alongside her, Comity could feel Fred tremble. Without collar and pipe or spectacles, he was a skinny little boy again, at the mercy of anyone on the station.

Comity could see her father standing on the verandah of Telegraph House, talking to the wiremen. She noticed how his suit hung loose on him these days, like a blanket over a tangle of barbed wire. There was a handkerchief clamped tight in one fist, and now and then he plucked on it with his teeth. He was despatching Cage and Amos and Hart to look for his daughter. The wiremen, home after twenty days in the saddle and sleeping on the ground, were intent on getting to the bathtub Loud Lulu was filling for them with pans of water.

When the Stationmaster saw his daughter emerge from the twilight, his face filled up with anger. It shrank her insides to the same size as the handkerchief. "Where have you been, girl?"

"I went following a honeybird, Papa. Looking for honey. I got lost. Luckily Fred *noticed* I was gone missing. *He* came looking." Did she mean to stress the words as she did? Surely not. And when had she become so adept at lying?

Loud Lulu began banging on the bathtub with the saucepan. The weary horses jostled each other. Somewhere, an owl complained of loneliness – *hoo-boo, hoo-boo*. Comity went and kissed her father and apologized if she had caused him any worry. The wiremen went to get their bath. The night settled like a campfire and a shower of sparky stars appeared. Sparks belched from the forge too, as Fred began pumping up the bellows.

"Leave it, fool. 'S'too late now," growled Smith, swinging the bridle half-heartedly at Fred. Thanks to Comity's fib, he had no excuse to thrash the boy. And anyway, people were looking. It would keep for another time.

CHAPTER SIX

Hogg

"You should tell that girl," said Smith. "Tell her to keep away from that blackfellah. His kind cannot be trusted."

Herbert Pinny tried hard to avoid conversations like this. He and Mary had had strong opinions on the Equality of Man. All men are precious in the eyes of God, and deserving of respect. It had been easy to say that in civilized Adelaide. It proved much harder in Kinkindele. "Not to be trusted" was as far as thinking had got there. No "comity" existed between black, white and ghan.

But Mary had insisted: while she lived in Telegraph House, all men and women would be treated as equals at Kinkindele.

Comity-of-nations had brought Mary and Herbert together. Both believed fervently that one day the nations of the world would come to respect and honour each other's laws and beliefs. As soon as that happened, war would shrivel and die. Peace would reign over all. It was why they named their daughter as they had. Comity had grown up firmly believing she would never go to heaven if she did not love foreigners.

She had no trouble at all liking Fred. She knew she *ought* to love and respect the ghans too. But they were just too frightening, what with their bandaged heads and dust-red eyes and foreign language; their no-smiles and their looking away. When gossip circulated of a white widow woman marrying a ghan cameleer and going to live in a ghantown, Mary Pinny had clapped her hands with joy, exclaiming, "Ah, *there* is comity!" And for one dreadful moment Comity had thought her parents meant to marry her off to a ghan. That was when she realized she probably ought to be called something different.

Little did Comity know it, but Herbert Pinny had been feeling much the same, ever since hearing of an attack on a telegraph station farther north. A spear in his back, his life blood spreading in a pool across some machine-room floor, Mr. Stapleton had tapped out a description of his Aboriginal attackers, before slumping insensible over his desk. Herbert had never told his wife about it, for fear of frightening her. But it had rather dented his faith in the comity of nations. There is nothing so denting to a man's ideals as the fear of a spear in the back.

"Camels in the yard!"

The shout made her flinch. But Comity no longer looked for her father to come out of his office to meet the cameleers. Five camel trains had called since the piano, and Comity had had to greet each one with lemonade and courtesy. She no longer made up excuses for her father's absence. She tried to look as if it was her job to take receipt of deliveries. She had come to recognize the cargoes, crated or wrapped in sacking: bottles of battery acid, parts for the generator, canned fish, porcelain wire-holders. (Guiltily she now knew why so many replacement wire-holders were needed: Fred had said what excellent spearheads they made when snapped smartly in half. She had told him off roundly – but watched open-mouthed with admiration as he shinnied up a telegraph pole and stole one, to make her a spear of her own.)

Today she could recognize among the cameleers the handsome ghan boy who had led the piano camel. He did not look away as all the others did, and even seemed ready to smile at her. But who was the white man in the ankle-length cotton coat and straw-boater hat?

Glancing at herself in the speckled mirror, Comity was taken aback to see how wild she was looking. Her nose and cheekbones were sunburned, and when she ran a brush through her hair, sand scattered across the floor, as well as a sprig of desert pea flowers Fred had stuck there the day before. When she opened the door, its frame was filled by the man in the duster-coat. He turned to the ghans and raised a hand. *"Kha safer walare!"* he called.

Then he turned back and ran his eyes over her like a flat iron over a shirt. His eyebrows rose halfway up his forehead. His mouth formed a tiny circle of mock astonishment, and he raised his hat with a gloved hand. "Quartz Hogg reporting for duty, ma'am," he said.

If Leonard had been less honest, it might never have happened. Months after resigning as deputy telegrapher at Kinkindele, he was astonished to discover that he was still receiving his salary. He assumed it was a mistake. He was not to know, of course, that Stationmaster Pinny had burned the letter of resignation or that Head Office thought he was still working there.

Many a young man would have been tempted to keep

the money. Not Leonard. He wrote to the Company returning their money in full and suggesting his letter of resignation must have been lost.

That was when the Company realized that Herbert Pinny had been struggling on single-handedly for six months. They hastily despatched a replacement.

So here was Quartz Hogg, deputy telegrapher, assigned for two years to share Henry Pinny's workload at Telegraph House.

"Papa, the replacement has—" was all Comity had time to whisper before Quartz Hogg burst into the machine room behind her and looked around him at his new workplace.

"Quartz O'Malley Hogg!" he declared, running his iron-grey eyes over Herbert's creased suit. "Your servant, sir. Your right-hand man. Your genie in a bottle. A winged Mercury to your Jove. Succour to your griefs and balm to your woes... A brandy would not come amiss."

Australian telegraphers are a particular breed of man. They are particularly particular about their appearance. Quartz Hogg carried a crystal-topped cane and wore spats, gloves and mutton-chop whiskers. His waistcoat was yellow tartan and his trousers and jacket green twill. He reeked of cologne. His luggage included a lady's riding crop, ten shirts, a corset, evening suit, cashbox, sugar, a pistol, an army rifle, cravats, and (apparently) two giant bedsprings. All this luggage lay ranged along the verandah now, like a well-stocked jumble sale. Recognizing the shape of a piano, Mr. Hogg threw back the sheet, pulled up a chair and began to play, pumping the loud pedal like the treadle of a sewing machine.

Herbert Pinny, trembling with nerves or outrage, breathed, "Leave that!" but Quartz Hogg was singing too loudly to hear.

The piano was hopelessly out of tune, the melody barely recognizable, but Hogg sang as though it were pitch-perfect. Months of silence shattered like grey glass. It was awful and shocking…and very slightly marvellous as well.

Astonished faces looked in at the window, and Hogg beckoned Amos and Hart and Cage and Smith to come on in. The sandy dust that had taken over the house was stirred up by stamping feet and the vibrations of the piano. It glittered in the low afternoon sun. Even the camel train watering their beasts at the trough looked back at the house in surprise.

Hogg leaped from song to song, sometimes abandoning one in the middle when a better one came to mind. The colour rising in his cheeks, he called for requests.

A smile twitched at Comity's mouth. She wondered if she dared ask for "Hang on the Bell, Nelly", which her mother had loved to sing.

"I have a request," said Herbert Pinny, his face ashen, his nose bleeding a little from pent-up emotion.

"What will it be, Mr. Pinny, sir?" asked the beaming Mr. Hogg, meaty hands poised over the keyboard.

"That you desist immediately."

Hogg lifted his foot. The damper silenced the humming piano wires. A damper fell on the party, too. Amos gathered up the dust sheet. Cage muttered something to Hart, and they picked up their hats off the dining table. Comity remembered that she must cook dinner for three and prepare a room for the new arrival, and that she did not know how.

Only Quartz Hogg was undismayed. He closed the piano lid with exaggerated care and squared up the candleholders. He appraised every face in the room with a flick of those grey, metallic eyes, then let them rest for the longest time on the Stationmaster. Herbert twitched his face aside. The wiremen filed out of the door.

"Right!" said Quartz springing to his feet. "When do we dine? Should I change for dinner?"

*

Hogg played cards with the wiremen, and they told him how glad they were of a new face; how these days Herbert Pinny never so much as came out of the house to be sociable, let alone invite them over.

"He's a shy man. I noticed as much," said Mr. Hogg.

He played dominoes with the land manager, who complained that no drink was allowed on the station, not so much as a bottle of sherry at Christmas time.

"He's a dry man. I noticed as much," said Mr. Hogg.

Exploring the forge, Hogg declared a passion for hunting. "When I was in the cavalry, they gave me a fine, big hunter. I miss her twixt my thighs. A man may make do with an indifferent wife, but he needs a good horse to be happy!" And Smith laughed, for Hogg seemed an unlikely huntsman in his tight trousers, the yolk-yellow waistcoat exaggerating his egg-shaped body.

He discussed ailments and remedies with the blacksmith, but the smith was not so easily won over.

"You talked to the ghans. In their own lingo." Smith made it sound like an accusation.

"Afghan War," said Hogg. "I was in Kabul." And instantly he soared in the smith's estimation, for he too had served with an army, and ex-soldiers are all brothers under the skin. "Those camel-fellahs say they fought on the side of the British. Mind you, what else would they say? That they fought against us?"

"Right. Right," said Smith. "Pinny lets that daughter of his go about with the yard boy. Blackfellah," said Smith.

"That one you mean?" said Hogg, and refocused his eyes on the distant figure of Fred, who was hoeing the vegetable patch.

Each man on the station was glad of Quartz Hogg's arrival, finding him a fellow after their own hearts. They might pity Mr. Pinny and respect his skill at Morse; still they found him a cold fish. It is hard to like a man who insists on keeping himself to himself.

"He is teaching me to play a tune on the piano!" Comity told Fred.

Fred made no reply. He had become oddly taciturn recently and Comity wondered if he was cross with her for spending time with the new telegrapher. Or perhaps he was worried that Mr. Hogg would keep a closer eye on the porcelain insulators.

She was ashamed – tried not to be, but was ashamed at the poor welcome her father had given Quartz Hogg. She could not fail to notice the differences between them. Once upon a time, her father had dressed as nattily as Mr.

Hogg – not quite so colourful in the waistcoat department, but abiding by the dress code of his profession. Even in the Outback, even under a slamming noonday sun, telegraphers kept up appearances. Now, though, Herbert Pinny's waistcoat was food-stained. His spats were pinked with dust. The toecaps of his shoes were scuffed. Even his hair hung lifeless and lank and ragged after Comity's efforts to cut it. His walking cane had been poked through the handles of the kitchen dresser to stop the doors swinging open, whereas Mr. Hogg's crystal-topped cane caught the sunlight, so that wherever he went, he was escorted by rainbows.

What would her mother have done? thought Comity. What kind of hospitality would she have offered this sociable, big-hearted man? Comity was out of practice with conversation, but there were other ways of being friendly. Her friendship with Fred, for instance, was built on stories. So Comity decided that tonight she would tell a story over dinner.

Choosing her moment, clearing her throat, she began, "In the Dreamtime, when the world was new, Bobbi Bobbi the Creator came down from the sky to see how everything was going along. As he glided hither and thither, he heard the sound of crying and came upon a crowd of people sobbing. 'What's the matter, little ones?' asked Bobbi Bobbi."

"Bobbi Bobbi?" said her father, emerging from his usual trance-like state. "What is Bobbi Bobbi?"

"He's a—" And to her horror, Comity realized that she had begun a story about a snake. As well as three plates of beans, she had inadvertently laid on the dinner table, in front of her father, a gigantic invisible snake. "He's a creator, Papa – like Byamee."

"Lord God Almighty created the world," said Mr. Pinny with an air of bewilderment.

"Yes. It is just a story Fred told me."

Her father frowned, considered, nodded. So Comity went on, treading (as it were) on snake eggs:

"*'What's the matter, little ones? I made you to be happy, not sad.'*

"*'But we are so hungry!' said the people. 'We have nothing to eat.'*

"*'What do you mean, you have nothing to eat? Did I not hang up bats in the trees and on the cliffs?'*"

"Bats?"

"Bats, yes, Papa.

"*'But we cannot catch them!' cried the people. 'We climb up. We get close and – rattle-fwoof – off they fly!' So Bobbi Bobbi thought, and then Bobbi Bobbi unhooked his scales and reached inside his chest and pulled out a rib.*"

"Scales?" said Mr. Pinny.

It seemed to Comity that an immense tiger snake was heaping its coils around the dining table, flickering its forked tongue over the dish of salt, yawning with disappointment at her lack of storytelling skill. She tried to think ahead through the story, to edit out all mention of snakes – which was hard, given that it involved Bobbi Bobbi winding himself around a mountain. Comity did the worst thing she could. She ploughed on.

"'Take my rib,' said Bobbi Bobbi. 'Use it to knock down the bats, and cook them in your campfires. This rib-stick will always come back to you, so it will never be lost. But never ever kill more than—'"

Quartz O'Malley Hogg broke wind – a noise so vulgar that the Rainbow Creator Snake was startled into silence. Hogg pushed his plate of beans, lentils and carrots away from him.

"Your daughter, Pinny, is plainly studying to keep house for a native. I trust she will not serve us bat for dinner?"

Herbert Pinny blinked, still startled by Comity breaking out in Story at all.

"Now, Pinny, old man, about that storehouse in the yard…" Hogg pinched fingerfuls of bread out of the new-baked loaf. "You have no objection if I stow some things in there?"

Next door, the machine rattled into life, and the room filled up with a swarm of words: CATTLE...RAILHEAD...BANKDRAFT...FODDER... The Stationmaster seized the excuse and was gone in a flash.

As the machine-room door closed behind him, Mr. Hogg, too, got up from the table. "These beans are blowing me up like a hot-air balloon, Miss Comity. You must change the menu. Allow me to help with the provisioning." And drawing his pistol, he went out of the door. There was a bang that set the piano wires trembling, and he returned carrying a chicken by its neck. With an exaggerated bow, he presented it to Comity like a bunch of flowers.

Feathery, still twitching, oozing blood from its staring eyes, the bird died in her lap. Comity looked across at the closed door of the machine room, and something inside her died, along with the chicken.

CHAPTER SEVEN

Invisible Mischief

Hogg made the stationery store his own, borrowing the key and forgetting ever to put it back. He clattered and banged about in there, and whatever it was he was doing, it engrossed him so much that he was often gone for hours. Somehow, Sunday morning prayers lapsed. Hogg's belongings left no room for Jesus. It was almost as if he thought he was the most important person around.

Little by little, Hogg let his duties lapse too. If a game of cards was not finished when his shift began, he stayed to finish the game. If a conversation with Smith turned to sport or war, he sat happily in the forge and told anecdotes about his days in the Army.

Far from being annoyed, Herbert Pinny was relieved. Solitude was his again and he clutched it round him like a shawl. Bad enough that his evenings were still jangled at dinner.

Quartz Hogg told the stories at table now – stories that grated on Herbert's beliefs and plain petrified Comity. He told of the fall of Kabul when the Afghans had promised to let the women and children go, then done unspeakable (well they *should* have been unspeakable) things, and left the women and children as dead as the cats on the cat tree. Then Hogg would break off and move over to the piano, merry as a kookaburra.

Comity, too, had stopped enjoying the musical interludes.

"He bounces me on his knee when he plays," she told Fred. But somehow saying it did not quite convey the violence of that thumping left foot or how the bouncing (and the toffee-sweet cologne in the man's hair) made her feel slightly sick. It sounded such a friendly thing to do: He bounces me on his knee.

Fred did not seem interested. He did not even stop hoeing the garden to answer her. The hoe-blade made a sharp hiss each time it cut into the sandy earth.

"Can we go to the railcar again?" Comity asked. She had been making a pot holder and a tablecloth for the carriage, and had set aside two chipped cups as well:

a thank you for letting her share his secret place. But Fred did not so much as look up. Was he sorry now that he had shown her his gunyah? "Are you awake-dreaming?" she asked, but got no answer.

Pocketing her hurt feelings, she went back to the house. As she did so, she spotted Hogg standing in the open doorway of the paper store, watching Fred. His big army pistol dangled from one finger.

Glancing in the mirror as she got indoors, Comity was startled to see that her cheeks were wet. It was annoying. Over the last few days she had often found herself unaccountably leaking at the eyes. In the dunny, in bed, standing at the stove poking the chicken bones into stock, or playing solitaire – anywhere she was unobserved, she would start to cry, all out of the blue. Rain from a cloudless sky. It made reading difficult, and without reading she found it hard to rise above things. The things Hogg talked about at dinner, and the Morse rattle of her heart kept her awake at night, too. She lay on her back, staring into the darkness. Mice moved through the walls of the house.

Or *was* it mice? Might it not be Wundas – those invisible mischief-makers who (Fred said) flew about stealing anything not nailed down? The kettle, for instance, and the garden twine had mysteriously gone missing from the kitchen.

At set of moon there was a rattling and scrabbling at the wall beside her, and she sat bolt upright in bed. "Fred? Is that you?"

A rattle, as of Morse, was tapped out against the window glass – an O? An F? A Q? "Mama? Is that you? *Say it! I cannot understand you!*"

The door of her bedroom slammed open and her father stood there in his nightshirt, wild-haired. "Wake up, Comity. You are dreaming."

She clung to him and clung to him, and told him how her mother was tapping at the window and that there were Wundas in the wall. He shushed her, flinched at the mention of his wife, and held her at arm's length as if she was on fire. And he did not believe one word.

"You were dreaming, child. It comes of eating meat after so long on beans."

And he would not go and look; would not, would not, *would not* go and look.

In the morning, the insect screen was gone from her bedroom window. It had been prised off the wooden frame.

So. Not her mother after all.

Comity was left to puzzle why, all of a sudden, Wundas had set their sights on Kinkindele Station and why winged invisible spirits of the Australian Outback wanted a kettle, twine and wire mesh.

My dear Cousins,

Here I am writing to you again. We have been
joined in our daily round by a Mr. Quartz Hogg who
is Father's new telegrapher. He can play the piano
and speak ~~Afgang Aphgan~~ Affgann because he was
in Cabool during the war. He made a good start
here but is rather lazy. Maybe it is homesickness.
The poor man misses the city something fearfull.
So if men are needed in Adelaide or somewhere,
we are quite reddy to let him go. You may tell
this to your important father, Super Intendent
Mr. Bligh.

   I hope you are well and clever as usual. We have
a summerhouse now with a sideways stove and seats.
It used to be a railway waggon till it hit a camel.
Your affecshunate cousin,
Comity

It was in mentioning the railway carriage that Comity
remembered the kettle on the stove, and thought how
useful it would be, in place of the missing copper one.
Now she would have to talk to Fred again, she told herself.
She threw back her shoulders and clenched her fists.

*

"I would like to go to the railcar again, please," she said, towering over him. Fred was kneeling down by the quince bushes, picking caterpillars off the fruit.

"Please go way. No more talk." Fred wriggled round so that his back was turned on her. "Please."

Comity wilted. "A Wunda stole my window screen last night," she offered, trying to pique his curiosity. But Fred's hands were shaking with fright, and she could see now that both Smith and Hogg had broken off from a game of mah-jong to watch.

"Five minutes. Under the house," said Comity in an undertone, and went back to the house. Settling herself on the verandah with a book, she was relieved to see a maze of prints made by bare feet beneath her bedroom window. Not Wundas, then. Wundas probably did not leave footprints, she supposed. Beneath her, a gentle scuffling hinted that Fred had arrived under the verandah.

"Not Wundas," said Fred's voice, beneath her feet. "Hogg want some things fetch to his gunyah."

"What kind of things?"

But Fred did not know. Every Aboriginal in Kinkindele seemed to know what was afoot…except for Loud Lulu and Fred. Now, when the Aboriginal mob sat in a circle to sing or eat or talk, the circle excluded Fred. It was a wall between him and the campfire. He was an outcast, and he had no idea why. He felt banished. It made the fear much worse.

"He shoot me if I talk with you," said Fred, and Comity was so shocked that she dropped her book. "He have big damn gun."

"I shall tell Father to dismiss him at once!"

A long silence followed which cast doubt on Comity's promise. Would Herbert Pinny really stand up to a man with a gun, who had seen battle in Afghanistan?

"What do you *think* Mr. Hogg is doing in the chapel?" she asked. "It makes a fearful noise."

"He build a Kadimakara," said Fred with his customary certainty. "The fellahs bring him things. I think he fix all things together. Build a Kadimakara."

"And that is? Tell me again?"

"Big damn monster. Fell down whoop-bang through the sky. Eat so many people down here he get fat. Not can get back up hole in sky. I show you. Big bone, yes? Bone of dead Kadimakara?"

She remembered. A single bone, as long as her leg, half embedded in the fossil rocks, up by the Dry Ocean. "For what? What for is he building one?" she breathed, feeling her heart run about her ribcage. "You are a noodle, Fred: how would a monster fit in the stationery store?" She shook her head and went on: "Anyway, I need a kettle.

Ours has disappeared, and I thought maybe—"

A rainbow scattered itself over her book, and she looked up to see Quartz Hogg grinning at her, running his eye this way and that along the verandah, twirling his crystal-knobbed cane.

"Are you so lacking in company that you must speak to yourself, Miss Comity?"

She snapped shut the ant-eaten book. "I read the words out aloud sometimes, Mr. Hogg. Just when people speak, you know? Just the parts inside the high-up commas."

He tilted the cane so that rainbows fluttered over her face like butterflies. It made her eyes skitter. She stiffened her resolve.

"Have you come to work your shift? Father will be glad. He gets so tired having to do everything himself."

But Hogg's gaze took in the sky, the view, the mah-jong board balanced on Smith's anvil, the birds in the trees, and he wrinkled his nose: there were better things on offer than work. "Is your father a hunting man, Miss Comity? Thought he might care for some sport this fine Sunday."

"I do not think he likes to kill things, Mr. Hogg."

"Now that is a shame. For every other telegrapher I know takes his rest on Sundays. Seems to me your father never leaves the house. Like Count Dracula."

"Naturally he comes out!" exclaimed Comity with what she hoped was a light laugh.

"Not as I hear it from the crew."

"Well, please to remember we are in mourning." It sounded like an excuse.

The smile never left Hogg's face. He snatched the book out of her lap in a movement so quick and insolent he might have been a child in school teasing a fellow pupil. Comity's letter to her cousins fell out; she had not been able to fetch an envelope for it from the stationery store.

"Excuse *me*!" she squeaked, as he began to read her letter. Hogg smiled even more broadly as he came to the mention of his own name, and the thinly veiled attempt to have him sacked.

As coolly as she was able, Comity got up and tugged open the swollen front door, wishing Hogg good day. But as soon as she was inside, she ran to the machine room and hauled on her father's arm. "Come! Please come! Come and tell Mr. Hogg to do some work. Come out and tell him you are not Count Dracula. You are not. He told Fred not to talk to me, and he cannot keep the chapel to himself and all the envelopes, and he is reading my…"

Her father's face reduced Comity to silence. It was so pale. His mouth was held in brackets of sore red eczema.

His eyes were pebbly grey and slow to soften at the sight of her.

Herbert Pinny stood up. Slowly, slowly, he put on his jacket and ventured as far as the verandah.

Quartz Hogg had not been idle since Comity's going indoors. He had gathered up the stones from around Mrs. Pinny's grave and piled them into two mounds at his feet. Twelve strides away, another had been placed to serve as a target.

"Game of pitch-and-toss, old peach?" he greeted his superior.

"Mr. Hogg, kindly return to your duties."

Hogg beamed. "Leave the door open, and we shall hear any incomings. All work and no play, Mr. Pinny…all work and no play." Everything in his manner was civil and cheery, polite and comedic. Everything in his meaning was snide and jeering. What was more, he had mustered Amos and Hart, Sankey, Cage and Smith to watch the game.

Both games.

Pitch-and-toss, and the taunting of Stationmaster Pinny.

At a distance, the stockmen, too, stood watching. Even the horses jinked in their paddock and looked across the yard.

Comity stared at the sacrilegious cairn of marker stones: Fred's tribute to her mother. "You took those off Ma's grave!"

"I did?" Hogg made great show of examining the stone in his hand. "You need fresh. The heathens have been daubing on these ones." His throw struck the target with a noise like a pistol shot.

Hart said, "Come along, Mr. Pinny. Your turn." Gentlest of the three wiremen, even Hart had been wound up like a cuckoo clock by Quartz Hogg and set to chirrup on time.

Sympathy does not live long among men. The team of hands working on Kinkindele resented the Stationmaster for shutting himself away from his only neighbours and making no effort to be sociable. The heart of Australia is a lonely enough place, without a man snubbing his workmates. Puzzled, offended and bored, they had been easily won over to Hogg's side.

"Your turn, Mr. Pinny," said Sankey. "Give it your best."

"Return to work everyone," suggested Herbert Pinny, in a voice cracked for want of use.

"It's Sunday, Mr. Pinny," said Cage.

Crack went the second stone.

Comity could not think which was worse – for her father to play pitch-and-toss with gravestones or to let Hogg humiliate him. She gave him an encouraging push –

"You can beat him, Father!" – and so she too sided with the enemy.

Herbert Pinny walked out into the middle of the yard, to the spot where his wife had died beneath the washing line. He picked up the stones painted to decorate her grave, and he flung them at the target. His hand shook. His head poked forward from his shoulders like a tortoise's. Impotent rage pulled his muscles taut. He tried not to look around him, but the trees seemed to jab at his eyeballs. The dust was made of God's funeral ashes, for surely God was dead or He would have put a stop to this.

Herbert stood in the Middle of Nowhere and flung stones at stones, when all he wanted to do was to beat them on Quartz O'Malley Hogg's skull until he had driven the man into the ground like a wash-post.

Fred, too, had been drawn to the pantomime in the yard. He stood staring at the painted boulders he had gathered from the bed of the creek. His lips moved in mumbled curses.

"You are in my eyeline, fellah," called Hogg and, without waiting for Fred to move, drew out his handgun from the back of his trouser band and pointed it at the boy's head. Fred ran like a rabbit, in stark terror, to the sound of laughter from men who had worked themselves up into that excitable frame of mind called bullying.

As Hogg threw the last of his stones, the sheet of paper that had lain beneath them blew across the yard and away under the fence – Comity's letter to her cousins. The one asking for Hogg to be recalled.

Herbert Pinny seized the chance to flee indoors, tripping up the steps in his clumsy haste.

That night, Hogg played the piano. The vibrations stirred up a colony of white ants infesting the woodwork. They swarmed out onto the glossy lid, and danced. Tossed up and down on Hogg's lap, her knees painfully cracking the underside of the keyboard, Comity fixed her eyes steadfastly on that strange constellation of ants. They formed themselves into loops and curves, knots and spirals – almost as if they were sending an SOS, a signal, a message. As the pencil through her topknot was shaken out and her hair collapsed, and splashed Quartz Hogg's exultant face, Comity knew very well what the ants were trying to tell her. She was a telegrapher's daughter, after all. She knew a code when she saw one.

*

"We have to get rid of Mr. Hogg," she told Fred next morning.

Fred put his head on one side and pretended to give this his measured consideration.

"Certainly indeed byallmean," he said, just a little too quickly.

CHAPTER EIGHT

Body Painting

Comity wrote down a list of Hogg's crimes.

Mr. Hogg is bilding a monster in the chapel.
Mr. Hogg keeps poynting his gun at Fred.
Mr. Hogg has stopped working.
Mr. Hogg plays the piano and it does not belong
to him.
Mr. Hogg makes people bring him things.
Mr. Hogg steels mail.

Herbert Pinny took out his blue pencil – the one he had
used in Adelaide to correct the messages scrawled by

ignorant members of the public. He began crossing through the crimes on Comity's charge sheet: one, two, three.

"Unlikely," he said.

"Not covered by Regulations," he said.

"Silliness." He even corrected her spelling – could not help himself. Once upon a time (it seemed to Herbert) he would have smiled at Comity's imaginings. Now it caused him nothing but anguish. That his little girl should be losing her grasp on the real world and straying into a maze of fantasies! How sad! How unutterably... His pencil came to a sudden stop.

"What do you mean, he steals the mail?"

"He took my letter I was writing to the Noxious Blighs!"

"Oh." The blue pencil crossed through the small matter of Comity's mail being stolen. She was not a member of the public: it did not matter.

Herbert would have liked to *add* to the list of crimes, as well as edit it. But it was not against Regulations for one man to humiliate another. It was not a sackable offence to be a loud and boorish oaf. And Herbert held himself partly to blame: a stationmaster's task is to instruct his staff in their duties...and Herbert had never instructed Quartz Hogg to do anything other than leave him in peace.

Which left only the matter of Fred.

Mr. Hogg keeps poynting his gun at Fred.

"Ask Mr. Hogg to come here, please, Comity," he said, and brushed the shoulders of his jacket and smoothed both palms over his raggedy hair.

"We here at Kinkindele believe in the comity of nations, Mr. Hogg," said the Stationmaster, a rivulet of sweat trickling down his temple.

Quartz Hogg twirled his cane. "That, Mr. Pinny, is because you do not know savages as I know savages. If you had fought in the Afghan War, you would know there are only two breeds of humankind in this world – the civilized and the murdering savage… Some of us are planning a dawn hunt tomorrow. Shall you join us?"

"On a working day? I forbid it. And, Mr. Hogg—"

"Oh, but then you do not care for the wide open spaces, do you, Mr. Pinny?"

Herbert Pinny writhed with rage and indignation. "Mr. Hogg! I did not summon you to talk of hunting. Your display of violence towards the yard boy was reckless and unChristian. It makes me doubt your suitability for this post. I shall be writing to the Company and instructing them—"

Hogg's smile showed more and more of his small, white, regular teeth. "And shall you tell them also that you allowed your dear late wife to operate the telegraph machine? Unqualified and without their permission?"

The mention of Mary landed among Pinny's thoughts like a stone, and scattered them.

Quartz Hogg had taken the measure of Herbert Pinny and the rest of the staff: he knew he was on safe ground. By pure luck, he had strayed into a kingdom ripe for the taking, so he had taken it, and though it might be a desert kingdom in the Middle of Nowhere, still that brought its own advantages. He patted the Stationmaster's cheek with more spite than affection and went back to the mysteries of the stationery store.

The making of monsters should rightly be left to those who live in the sky. But the Devil-Devil was built by a mere man. The man gave it quills and fists, eyes and teeth, claws and scales and lungs like bellows. He stuffed it with rage…then found he had too little magic to bring the thing to life. There it lay, stretched out along the ground like a dead camel but twelve times as big. In his frustration, he kicked it – kicked it again, over and over, until fur and fingers and feathers were scattered all around.

Then the Devil-Devil stirred. It pulled itself onto its hands and haunches and stood up. The man could run – but the Devil-Devil could bound, sprint, run without tiring. It quickly caught up with the man who had built it. It tore him to pieces.

That used up no more than a pinch of the Devil-Devil's fury, and so it lifted up all of its four noses and snuffed the wind. From every direction, the wind brought it the stench of human wickedness.

Ever since that day, the Devil-Devil has chased anyone wicked. Villains have tried hiding, building traps, arming themselves with weapons or magic… But nothing can stop the Devil-Devil once it has picked up the scent of a wrong-doer.

"Please don't let's summon the Devil-Devil! It might eat us!" said Comity, round-eyed with fright. "It might eat everybody here!"

"Nah. Devil-Devil chase only the bad people," Fred assured her. "Eat Hogg alonely. Maybe Smith."

"But if we call up the Devil-Devil and it tears Mr. Hogg to pieces, then we're wicked too! It will eat us too!" Comity could picture the Devil-Devil sprinting across the landscape towards Kinkindele, teeth bared. The ghost-gum trees seemed to have pictured it too, for they had sweated their pale sweat and their barks were stripy with white rivulets of gum. Fred scraped up a fistful, and began grinding it in an earthenware bowl last used by Mrs. Pinny to make bread-and-butter pudding. "You said get rid."

"*Frighten* him, I meant! Frighten him so much he won't dare stay! Tuckonies would do, I'm sure!" So they settled for summoning impish Tuckonies instead, and Fred showed Comity how to apply the magical body paint he had made from ghost-gum resin.

Comity watched, mesmerized by the antlike procession of tiny white dots edge-to-edge on black skin. The dots marched, single-file, over Fred's ribs and collarbones. It took infinite patience, and he was left-handed so could not decorate his left arm; nor could he reach his back. So Comity carried the magical symbols over his shoulder and down the vertebrae of Fred's spine. She tried to remember the patterns formed by those white ants on the lid of the piano. Across Fred's forehead she wrote the Morse for *HELP*. Then she stripped to her spencer and drawers, and Fred decorated her body too.

Clad in the sacred dance-patterns of the ant-people, they danced now, to summon up magic. Comity copied

91

Fred's every invented step, every guttural, grunted word. But his Aboriginal chanting did not rhyme, and Comity – heir to a great many fairy tales – was convinced it should. So she asked Fred what the words meant that he was chanting, and then made up her own version.

"Bird and bear and sun and breeze,
Rock and water, fire and trees,
Whistle up the Tuckonies."

Fred was enchanted by the idea of Aboriginal magic being spoken in English, not to mention rhyming.

"Rock and water, fire and trees,
Whistle up the Tuckonies!"

They could not quite agree what favour they should ask of the dwarfish little trickster-spirits. A snake in Hogg's bed? A scorpion among his beans? Should he be mobbed by bats, carried off by an eagle, or kept awake forever by invisible kookaburras?

A vortex of dust about as tall as Fred and shaped like a spinning top spun its way across the desert, scattering dust and dry grass. Comity clung to Fred's arm. "Is that one there?"

It had never occurred to Fred before that these familiar dust eddies might be stirred up by Tuckonies. He was more than happy to believe it.

"Eye of newt and toe of frog,

Frighten horrid Mr. Hogg," chanted Comity. She was improvising now.

"*Make him want to go back home.*

Make him leave us quite alone."

For two hours Fred and Comity, apparelled in magic patterns, danced under the ghost-gums, and watched for eddies of dust that might mark an army of Tuckonies mustering. For two hours they danced, then they returned to the station. Were the animals in the paddock twitching more than usual? Surely, they were. Surely they could sense magical mischief close by? The children watched for Hogg to burst from his gunyah, sobbing and wailing, ooching and ouching as invisible imps tormented him.

Nothing.

They waited till night stole the colour out of the flowers, and bats took the place of birds, and the light of Smith's forge went out and lamps were lit in Telegraph House.

Nothing.

"What now?" asked Comity, disappointed and weary from an afternoon spent dancing in the sun. Her skin was as itchy as if white ants were swarming all over her.

But Fred had melted out of sight, too afraid of Hogg to be seen anywhere near Comity.

*

"Where is Lulu?" Comity asked at dinner.

The laundress was not exactly reliable. Sometimes she would do the laundry three times a week, swooping into the house and stripping the beds, like a vulture stripping carrion. Then for three weeks she might declare everything too clean to wash. She might demand the shirt from a man busily at work and, if he refused to give it up, stand at a distance shrieking, "Man smell! Dirty boy!" until he relented. Or she might return his long johns to him with the leg ends sewn up. She was an oddity as laundresses go, but a familiar sight around and about the station, talking to herself or smoking her pipe.

Now Lulu seemed to have disappeared. Had the Tuckonies kidnapped the wrong person? Or had she been snatched inside the stationery store and eaten by the Kadimakara? "Where's Lulu?" she asked again.

Her father shifted his cup on its saucer. "Mr. Smith felt he had to dismiss her."

Comity was stunned. "Can he do that? What did she do?"

Herbert Pinny busied himself with his boiled egg, but Quartz Hogg winked at Comity across the table, raised an invisible glass to his lips and rolled his eyes. Comity hated the gesture, but she understood it. She did not quite know why alcohol was wicked, but then she had never seen anyone drunk. Hard liquor was forbidden on the station. Hard liquor was an abomination to her father. If Loud Lulu had partaken of strong drink, she had forfeited her place at Kinkindele for ever.

"Where did Lulu get strong drink?" Comity asked. "How would she?" Questions danced through Comity's head, along with the knowledge that now she would have to launder her own bedsheets to get out the stains of body paint.

"Never fear, Miss Comity," said Hogg. "We shall find another woman to wash the laundry. We cannot have your pretty hands made red by washing soda. Soon enough you will make some man a wife, and though a man out here may want many things of a wife, a washerwoman don't come high on the list."

A trapdoor opened in the bottom of Comity's stomach. She knew Hogg was teasing – making fun of her. Marriage might be years away – years and years. But suppose Mr. Hogg *never* went away, just stayed and stayed until she really was a grown woman and he had made Kinkindele his own private kingdom?

Her father's teaspoon, scraping the shell of his empty egg, went through it with a crunch.

"My term of duty will finish long before Comity reaches womanhood, Mr. Hogg," he said, between clenched teeth.

"She shall be married among family and friends in Adelaide, and, please God, to some man of a hard-working and honest disposition. Do you suppose I would cast her adrift in this appalling wasteland?"

It was an outburst wrung from him like juice from a lemon and twice as bitter. He picked up his bread knife and it seemed, for a moment, as if he might actually throw it at Hogg. His colour had changed alarmingly and he tugged his celluloid collar away from its studs, choking on anger. Then he went to the machine room and Comity went to her bed. She heard Quartz Hogg leave the house, whistling to himself – a jaunty little tune intended to prove that Pinny had not startled him in the least. She heard the door of the stationery store open and close.

Tears trickled from the corner of her eyes into her ears, and Comity had no idea if they were tears of sorrow or happiness. She hated quarrels, shouting, unpleasantness – but at least her father had stood up for her! He meant to keep her safe and to take her home to Adelaide one day! About that, too, Comity did not know whether to laugh or cry. Adelaide had faded to somewhere only half real: somewhere she might have read about in a storybook.

The door of the stationery store opened and shut again: Hogg was back in the yard. "*You there, jacky!* You lurking, are you, boy? You a-skulking? Thought I told you: no abo's in the yard after sundown. Skip."

A pistol shot rang out so loudly that the horses in the barn shrieked and clattered their hoofs against the barn wall.

CHAPTER NINE

Widow-maker

Comity mixed the pituri juice into the lemonade using a fork, and watched it swirl around the glass, opaque and grey. She fished out two lemon pips.

"What if it changes the colour of the lemonade?" she asked.

"He think it some another juice," said Fred, mashing more leaves between two rusty spoons. The few drops of liquor he got from the leaves did not look enough to discolour a sheet of paper. A fly plunged into the lemonade, obstinately determined to drown. Comity fished it out with the fork. It spun round and round on its back on the kitchen table, rattling its wings and wriggling its legs.

She imagined it was Quartz Hogg and swatted it with a letter from Aunt Berenice.

Of course, it would take more than a letter to swat Hogg. Her nervousness of the deputy telegrapher had turned to loathing the moment he had loosed off a pistol at Fred. The bullet had sunk into the stable wall so close to Fred's arm that splinters of wood had embedded themselves in his elbow. It was plain Hogg no longer cared whether he missed or hit Fred. Anyone who would do that deserved to come to a bad end, and as soon as possible.

By the look of him, Fred had spent all night grinding pituri leaves. The spoons came from his railcar, where he had run in terror from Hogg's pistol. Lying within the railcar, Fred had thought he could never go back to the Repeater Station – never give Hogg another chance to kill him. The Law offered no protection to an Aboriginal yard boy, and besides the Law was a hundred miles away. The Stationmaster would not leap to Fred's aid. What? Mr. Pinny tell Hogg to surrender his gun? No. Quartz Hogg had made himself king of Kinkindele.

But towards dawn Fred had realized he could not stay up at Miser's Gorge. He was chained to Repeater Station Number Four: by memories of Mrs. Pinny, by Comity's friendship, and by having all his ancestors buried on Kinkindele land. No, he must go on tending the garden, working the forge bellows and sweeping the verandah, while Hogg watched and grinned and pointed his big old pistol...

Unless he could be got rid of.

So while Hogg went for his regular morning expedition, shooting things "to keep his aim sharp", Fred raked out the wood ash from the stove and mixed it with the juice of ground-up pituri leaves, the way Aboriginals drugged emus before killing and roasting them. Not that roast Hogg was on the menu. He would return from his hunting trip with a raging thirst and drink the doped lemonade, then fall asleep in his bedroom, slipping gently into unconsciousness. Then they would take all his guns away and bury them and drop the Army pistol down the dunny and tell everyone Hogg was drunk, so he would be sacked like Loud Lulu and instantly sent away.

Comity added the final trickle of leaf juice to the speckled lemonade and Fred returned the rusty spoons to his dillybag. Comity swept the mess of leaves out-of-doors and over the edge of the verandah...

...onto the very toes of Hogg's boots.

"I thought you were out in the buggy, Mr. Hogg," said the criminal, caught red-handed.

"Forgot my hat, sweetheart."

His rather large and sticky-out ears were catching the

sun, and with his crystal-topped cane, Hogg looked like an affable wizard about to do magic. The thought went through Comity: *We cannot do this.*

Then Hogg looked over her head, caught sight of Fred, and his top lip curled. "That dog come sniffing again?"

"Come for the laundry, Mr. Hogg," said Comity, her heart hardening to ice. "His mama is going to do it in place of Lulu. There is lemonade fresh made." And she poured it for him, smiling her best smile, and watched him drink it down. (She knew she must make a show of liking Hogg, even though inwardly she wanted to swat him like a blowfly.) She poured him another glass.

He smacked his lips, trying to identify the strange but not unpleasant taste.

"You adding chasers now for my delectation, beautiful?" And he arched an eyebrow at her, as he might at a barmaid in Darwin.

Fred meanwhile scurried about, back bent, head down, snatching up anything that was, could be, might be washable. He left with such a load of sheets, cloths and clothing that he had to charge the door three times over to squeeze through it.

Not the smallest change was visible in Hogg. He fetched his hat and headed out again to the pony and trap. It had grown to look like some Roman chariot, bristling now with rifles, spears, woomeras and the umbrella Hogg used for a parasol. The sun glinted on the crystal buttons of his waistcoat as he bowled out of the yard.

Fred and Comity sat on the pile of "washing" in among the eucalyptus trees and wondered what they had done. They could not bring themselves to speak. Besides, their thoughts were running free across the surrounding countryside, following the man in the yellow waistcoat.

This was not what they had planned. Perhaps this was better, though. Perhaps the concoction of pituri and wood ash would tip Hogg out of the trap onto his head and leave him helpless as a drugged emu, for the crows and dingoes to eat. Perhaps he would drive into a ravine or, hallucinating, imagine he saw castle turrets and set off to find them, and disappear into the red desert, never to be seen again. Perhaps he would think himself an eagle and climb to the top of a tree and hurl himself off it, arms outstretched.

"That would be like us killing him!" said Comity.

Warrior Fred could not see a problem with that.

…There again, at any moment Hogg might come bowling back through the gate, fit as a flea – and then what?

After a while, Comity began to think about the pony and trap. She thought how the trap was the property of the British-Australian Telegraph Company – and found she could not care what became of it. But the horse? Starbuck was a nice horse. Her mother had named him after some horse in *Moby Dick*, and Starbuck had done nothing to deserve death between the shafts of a wrecked trap or lying at the bottom of a ravine with his legs twitching.

And suppose Hogg did disappear into the red desert? Would she not spend every waking minute waiting for him to crawl, living, through the kitchen door or walk, dead and ghostly, through her bedroom wall? She mentioned her fears to Fred.

"We find him. We finish him," said Fred doubtfully.

"We find him anyway," said Comity.

He was not hard to find. Quartz Hogg had not got far at all before the effects of the pituri juice had filled him with the seven colours of the rainbow, deep spiritual bliss, a violent need to pee, then the craving to sleep. Starbuck, feeling the reins go slack, had come to a stop and then, as the day's heat grew, headed back towards the station. Thirst and a patch of sweet grass had sidetracked him by the stream, and this is where Comity and Fred spotted him, from the top of Goat Ridge.

Quartz Hogg was slumped over the side of the trap, his hat gone and his head puce from hanging upside down. In the time it took them to run from Goat Ridge to the river, he had not stirred a muscle, but his choked snores were a strong hint he was not dead.

"Now what?" said Comity.

Seeing the man play pitch-and-toss with painted stones from the grave, Fred had wanted to heave rocks at him. Seeing him bully her father, seeing the splinters in Fred's elbow, Comity had wanted to strangle Hogg with piano wire from the Hapsburg Beale. But this grunting, helpless, upside-down snorer looked more emu than villain, and emus are not hateful.

Then Fred looked around him and gave one of his sharp, decisive nods. "Tree can choose," he said, and toppled Hogg out of the cart.

Comity was sure Hogg would wake long before they reached the widow-maker. Each holding a wrist, they were dragging him over spinifex clumps, stones and brittle twigs, filling up the seat of his trousers and loosening his boots. A crystal button popped off the yellow waistcoat.

Fred put it in his dillybag for a trophy.

The tree on the nearby hillock was majestically tall. Its bare branches cast shadows like rheumatic fingers.

Come closer, children, whispered the shadows. *Rest here, out of the sun.*

Wherever a branch sprouted sparse, blue leaves, it cast furry patches of shade that looked inviting in the great heat of noon. The last few yards rose steeply upwards and Comity wanted to stop short, but Fred insisted on dragging Hogg as far as the tree trunk itself – right in under the canopy of withered branches – despite his lifelong fear of the widow-maker.

All that remained was to run, leaving the tree to pass sentence on Quartz Hogg and to carry it out on their behalf.

They paused at the bottom of the hillock. Should they leave without knowing the outcome, or stay and watch?

Fred said they should dance. Comity tried to copy the tilt of his body, the lopsided shifting of weight. Their shadows lapped and overlapped as they danced their invented ritual dance and chanted their invented magic chant and watched for the widow-maker to pronounce sentence.

An old blue gum tree drops its branches without warning or pity – branches so heavy and huge that a man foolish enough to sleep away noon in their shade can wake up as flat as unleavened bread and deader than the Ancient Egyptians.

"Come here and help us, Tuckonies,
We beg you on our bended knees.
Lo, a man beneath you lies.
Shall he live or shall he die?"

Fred was tireless in his dancing. It absorbed him completely. Comity, too, should have emptied her head, but instead she watched the widow-maker. She watched it so intently that her eyeballs got dry, and the brightness of the sky made her head pound. At any moment – at any moment – any second now a branch would break with enough noise to rouse every bird for miles around into the sky in a panic of wings. Any second – at any moment – any second now, the noise would make her jump out of her skin. Other thoughts must have crept into her head too, because suddenly she heard herself ask:

"What shall we do about the Kadimakara? After." Fred kept on dancing. He did not appear to have heard. "If we let it out of Jesus' gunyah, it will eat everybody."

"We burn Jesus' gunyah," said Fred with a resolute nod of his head.

"But it's the property of the British-Australian Telegraph Company! And Mama's Bible is in there!"

"We give poison meat," said Fred.

The sun was hot on the top of Comity's head. She had been in such a hurry leaving the station that she had not put on her hat, and dancing had wrung so much sweat out of her that the very bones of her arms felt dessicated: at any moment they might snap and fall away from her like the branches off a tree. Fred had said that the Tuckonies were invisible, and yet now, when Comity looked up at the crown of the widow-maker, she thought she could see them – splodges of yellow light, jumping along the boughs, dancing in time to the thump of her heart. Even Starbuck the pony, bitten by flies, was dancing between the shafts of the trap: an unhappy, sweaty, fly-blown dance.

The thready ticking of her pulse sent a Morse message to the distant machine room of her brain:

RISE ABOVE THIS COMITY STOP

THOU SHALT NOT KILL

"Mama does not want us to do this," she said.

Fred had his eyes shut. He was dancing as he would at a corroboree, under a heatless moon, his ribcage working like the bellows in the forge, his bare feet and legs grey with dust. He had learned Comity's chant and made it his own, splicing the words together until they sounded like a foreign language, a magic language. He could not hear her. In any case, thought Comity, she could not make him go in under the tree again when at any moment… No. She would have to do it herself.

She ran at full tilt, jumping the gnarled shadows and grabbing Hogg's feet. His shoes came off, and she sat down hard. His socks dangled off the ends of his feet. *"Get up. Get up, Mr. Hogg. Got to get up now."* She picked up one of his hands, and felt the pudgy softness of his palm, the prickle of the hair at the wrist. Fred appeared at her shoulder. Now, when the branch fell, he too would be killed, and it would all be her fault. Her eyes filled with liquid. Now even her eyeballs were sweating!

"We doing what?" asked Fred, grabbing Hogg's other hand and pulling. Hogg rose into a sitting position between them. With his head hanging backwards and his eyelids slightly open, he appeared to be looking at them.

"Mama says not to," said Comity.

And, miraculously, that was enough. Fred had danced himself into a trance under the sun, and still the branches had not dropped. The widow-maker had ignored him. But this marvellous girl, who could chant in rhyme, had been visited by the spirit of Mrs. Pinny, and Mrs. Pinny had called a halt. Instantly Fred joined Comity in dragging Hogg clear of the blue gum tree. Arms at full stretch above his head, Hogg's shirt came untucked; his trouser belt broke. He weighed as much as a camel.

BANG. A noise like the sky breaking its back. An avenging angel had surely struck his wing against the ground, because suddenly Fred and Comity were enveloped in feathery blue leaves. The widow-maker had let drop a branch. They stopped stock-still, waiting for the pain of death to seize them... But all that came was a stinging soreness like dozens of paper cuts up and down their arms and shoulders. Hanging between them like a dead sheep, Quartz Hogg was unscathed: their own bodies had protected him from the splash of leaves. Where, a moment before, he had lain on the ground, half a ton of dry timber lay part-sunk into the hard earth, shedding bark and insects and invisible Tuckonies. Comity and Fred could still feel the vibration through the soles of their feet.

All the short drive home they were silent. Fred took the cartridges out of Hogg's shotgun and put them in his dillybag, but nothing was said, except by Quartz Hogg, who had begun to mumble and groan and cough, choking on his own snores. Now and then, an arm twitched involuntarily and caught them a blow or landed between them on the buckboard, the fingers opening and closing, opening and closing.

*

Amos and Hart took charge of Hogg, glancing furtively towards Telegraph House as they lifted him down from the trap. Clearly they thought Hogg was drunk, which suited Comity very well (though she could not imagine how they thought he had come by alcohol, way out here in the Bush). They did not want the Stationmaster to see him drunk and dismiss him, so they put him to bed in their own quarters. Smith the smith, finding Hogg's shoes in the trap, polished them up himself, using saddle soap.

Quartz Hogg woke with a headache, a pain in his neck and a taste in his mouth like boiled goanna, but with no recollection at all of the outing. It was as if a tree had fallen across his memory and obliterated one whole day.

"You are lucky the children found you," said Sankey. "I knew a wireman fell from a pole one time. Broke a leg. Lay out in the sun. Dead by sunset. Sun can do that."

Quartz Hogg contemplated his good luck. He contemplated the little empire of Kinkindele and how easily it had fallen into his hands. He contemplated where he might stow Herbert Pinny after he took over Telegraph House, and how he could guarantee the man went on working away in the machine room. After all, Kinkindele Repeater Station must continue to run smoothly.

The Stationmaster had a great many weaknesses – a fear of the outdoors, grief, goody-goodness and, of course, the girl. Yes. The girl was the key. Comity was the key, and the thought brought a smile to his sun-cracked lips. A brush with death gives a man a greater appreciation of life. Everything was coming along nicely in the stationery store. His lucky escape called for a celebration.

He summoned Herbert Pinny to his bedside and declared, "Time for a *party*, old peach."

CHAPTER TEN

A Place of Safety

"*Go?* What do you mean, *go?*" said Comity.

Her father peeled the spine off *Poems: Jean Ingelow.*
He extracted a double strip of ribbon hidden there long
before. "Go and stay with Fred's people. He can take you.
The pony and trap are ready. It is for two days only." He
gave her the ribbon. Sewn into it were six dollar coins.

"Why? Why must I go? Fred does not *have* people,
Papa. Fred is just Fred."

"Two, three days only, Comity. Oblige me in this.
Ghantown, then. Go to the ghantown at Calgo Crossing.
The Afghans are a hospitable people, I believe."

"But Mr. Hogg says they chopped everybody up in the

war and burned their babies and cut their insides up and put out their eyes and—"

"What nonsense. Mr. Hogg intends a party, and I do not think it fitting for you to be here." Then his face shut down, fretful and angry, though his eyes continued to plead with her: *Go, Comity. Go. Two days is little enough to ask.*

He could not mean it. What was so dangerous about a party? Comity dimly recalled parties back in Adelaide – singing and cake, odd-smelling relations, borrowed dinner services and a clutter of extra chairs; her mother doling out sandwiches and questions and jokes. Parties were happy things, surely, not grounds for running away? Yes, she could see that parties involved more than two people together in the same room. But why did *Comity* have to go away, just because Herbert Pinny had a horror of crowds? And if parties were dangerous, how much more dangerous was sleeping on the ground among spiders and snakes and ants and dingoes and perentie lizards?

Perhaps her father was planning to confront Hogg about his uppish, lazy ways and give him notice to leave, and expected to be shot dead by the bestial Hogg and did not want his daughter to see it! Or perhaps he had found out about the Kadimakara in the stationery store and meant to do battle with it, like Saint George with the dragon.

"Come with us if you are…" (She must choose her words carefully.) "…worried."

"Nonsense. How can I leave my post? You should know better than to ask it…"

"It will be dark soon, Papa! It is almost night! What if Fred and me get lost? What if we get eaten by wild dogs!" She followed her father around the house, tugging on his jacket, trying to tell him what a bad idea it was. Mr. Pinny meanwhile, picked up a blanket from the bed, a loaf, a water bottle, a dinner knife, the maimed copy of *Poems: Jean Ingelow.*

Fred hovered by the door, standing sideways on because he was not part of the conversation, wondering how to say no to the bossman. He had never been to a ghantown and he did not mean to start now. Did the Stationmaster not realise how much the ghans hated the Aboriginals, and vice versa? He tried to be clever and perspicacious – to read the heart of Mr. Pinny and find out just what he was afraid of. But Mr. Pinny was curlew-cursed and who can read the heart of a creature that spends its life cowering at the back of a cave?

Comity took the badly-packed bundle of things from her father and threw them on the ground. She actually stamped her foot. "I will *not* go to the ghantown! I hate ghans." It was a terrible thing to say. She half expected her father to stagger backwards clutching his heart. "Also, Fred does not know the way!"

Herbert Pinny bit his lip and made it bleed. "Is that so, Frederick?"

"Verily, yes sir," said Fred, quick as a snake's whistle.

A rictus of confusion and pain twisted the Stationmaster's face. He put on his jacket. "Very well. It seems I must take you." He looked around the room as if for objections to him leaving. The room was silent but for the sound of his own fingers clicking – a nervous habit he had developed without noticing.

"It is the Kadimakara, isn't it?" said Comity, gently taking hold of her father's hand.

Fred gasped and lifted his bare feet as though the secret spilled was hot liquid.

Pinny turned on his daughter a pair of uncomprehending eyes.

The girl was forever picking up Aboriginal words. She brought them home as other children brought home beetles or dead birds. How pleased Mary would have been. How intensely irritating he found it.

"If you say so," he said sharply. "We shall go to Calgo Crossing. Tomorrow I shall return here alone and assess the…damage." And shouldering the blanket bundle, gritting his teeth, he opened the door.

*

The whole of Australia unfurled in front of Herbert Pinny. The evening sun cast prodigious shadows – black tongues lolling. A tidal wave of insect-sound broke over his head, left him gasping, unable to breathe. It was all he could do to climb into the buggy. He sat on the buckboard, picked up the reins, then sat staring at his hands, which were shaking uncontrollably. The tremors reached the pony's mouth, and Starbuck shuffled uncertainly: was that the signal to go or stop? The flies had heard the remarkable news – *Herbert Pinny has stepped out of doors!* – and their curiosity settled on him in black clouds, trying to see up his nose, inside his ears, behind his lashes, to map every fold of his landscape and drink the blood off his bitten lip.

Herbert did not want the gardening boy in the cart with them – sitting behind him, within a hand's reach of Hogg's weapons. Minutes before he had been willing to entrust his daughter to Fred's safekeeping. Now he was afraid of being stabbed in the back with a porcelain-headed spear. After all, what did he really know about Fred?

There again, Fred probably knew the terrain better. What if they strayed off the track and got lost? Herbert could not navigate by the stars. How would he ever have learned? Fearing them as he did.

Even as Pinny steered Starbuck through the gate, evening congealed into dusk. An hour later, the temperature plummeted. In place of the flies came stars. A thousand thousand burned their way into sight, like white-hot needlepoints threatening his eyes. Millions of maggot stars squirmed out of the dung-dark sky and clung there wriggling. Not for long.

"Are you all right, Papa?"

The whole sky began to revolve: a dizzying maelstrom of fathomless water and nothing holding it in place, nothing to keep it from falling on him.

"What's the matter, Father?"

Now it began to fall. The stars began to plummet towards him; a hailstorm of stars. He was being pelted with stars. They would pulverize him, sink deep into his flesh, pin him to the ground and bury him. Lower and lower his head sank. He let go the reins and cupped his hands over his eyes to shut out the cataract of stars, the avalanche of stars, the edgeless Everywhere that so horrified and terrified him. "Mary. Mary. Help me, Mary," he said.

Comity leaned over to take the reins and encountered clenched hands as cold as liver. When she looked across, her father's face was so white that it gleamed in the dark.

As she swung the pony and trap around, he reeled sideways and his cheek brushed hers, clammy cold. "We should go back, Papa."

"Yes! I have changed my mind. I cannot desert my station. What was I thinking of? You are quite old enough to go on your own. Are you? I don't know!"

And he did not. All power of decision, all resolve, all common sense had been pelted out of him by the hail of stars. They started back in silence the way they had come, Comity driving, Pinny with his head almost between his knees. They had travelled one hour away from a party. They travelled another hour back home, to save Pinny from the dark.

"Fred has a railcar up near Miser's Creek. We could go there, Papa."

"Very well. Yes. Do as you see fit. Yes. Go there. Two days."

As they drove into the barn, he jumped down from the cart and twisted his ankle but still ran all the way, stumbling over the unmarked mound of his wife's grave and into Telegraph House.

"What do we do?" said Comity. Her first choice would have been to cry, but if ever a situation needed rising above, this was it.

Fred's gaze was fixed on the stationery store, for he had convinced himself this was the night Quartz Hogg meant to let loose the Kadimakara.

"Can we find your railcar in the dark?"

"Byallmean," said Fred unenthusiastically.

"Or we could sleep under the stars?" said Comity.

"Three dog night," said Fred, picking up the Stationmaster's forgotten jacket and slipping his arms into it. Comity had no idea what "three dog night" meant, but it conjured pictures of teeth and slaver and glittering dingo eyes. Perhaps they should simply creep back into the house and sit out the party in Comity's bedroom.

"Burn it dead," said Fred suddenly with a decisive jerk of his head. "Yeah verily. You got kerosene?"

Comity had a horror of fire. Living in a thatched house in a country seared to kindling by the sun, she often lay in bed planning her escape if ever she woke to find Telegraph House ablaze. Now Fred was bent on setting light to a wooden stationery store in the middle of the compound, to kill the monster inside. She asked herself what her mother would think, but that was ridiculous. If Mary Pinny had still been alive there would be no monster: no monster, no Quartz O'Malley Hogg, no panic, no choices to make.

Her father expected them to be gone, so Comity and Fred drove the trap into the barn and hid there. The lights were on in Telegraph House and the party underway. Hogg was thumping the piano keys so hard that the china teacups on the dresser were tinkling. Someone had laid hands on a penny whistle but not the knack of playing it. Amos was playing comb-and-paper. Hart was rattling a pair of spoons.

Twice Comity heard Hogg shout for her to come and join in: he must think she was still in the house, sulking in her room. Instead, she and Fred were busy unhooking the spirit lantern that hung by the forge. On every side, the dry straw bales piled against the walls ticked like clocks. A rat moved about overhead. The night was loud with insects. Outside, the cattle mooed, and chewed the cud: they were restive, unsettled by the music, perhaps, or the presence (unusual at night) of Aboriginals standing among the gum trees, watching. Watching for what?

When Fred lit the lamp with his flint lighter, a dozen lizards on the barn wall flinched. A rising moon was keeping a watchful eye on the two skulking children.

"No," Comity said. "We cannot burn it. We will only make it angry and then it will kill everybody."

But Fred had risen above the dust-cloud of doubt into a realm of pure, clean fear. When the piano fell silent, his sharp ears could pick out a soft gurgling noise within the store. The monster's hungry belly rumbling, for sure. Here was a monster built of barrel hoops, window screens, pots, pans and kettles, whose fiery dreams leaked smoke through the roof of Jesus' gunyah. And it was up to Fred to kill it.

Holding the lantern inside one flap of the Stationmaster's jacket, he crept out of the barn and across the yard. If the door was unlocked, he would throw in the lamp and allow it to smash at the monster's feet. Poor evicted Jesus would surely do the rest, fanning the flames from his throne in the sky. Jesus was good with lamps, after all: *The Light of the World* picture proved that.

Fred reached for the door of the store, fully expecting it to be locked. He had just gripped the handle when it moved of its own accord within his hand and the door swung towards him. What Fred saw was not the Kadimakara.

It was Hogg.

That was why the piano had fallen silent: Hogg had stepped out of the house and gone to the store to fetch something. The two stared at each other.

"Now there's a garment I recognize," said Hogg. His fat, pink fingers stroked the lapels of Pinny's borrowed jacket. Then his hands closed into a fist and he pulled Fred sharply towards him, all but lifting him off the ground. The lantern fell to the ground. "I see you are true to your breed, jacky. Thieving is your stock-in-trade."

Kicking the store door shut, and dragging Fred with him, he fairly trotted back towards the party. A sharp high noise of triumph came from him, like the squeal of a piglet. "*Look here! Come see!*" Men and Aboriginal women spilled out of Telegraph House.

Comity, frozen with indecision, stood in the shadow of the barn and watched the horror unfold. At every moment she expected her father to emerge onto the verandah like everyone else, but he did not. Inside the house the furniture had been pushed back against the wall to make room for dancing. By accident, or on purpose, it had blocked the door of the machine room, and imprisoned Herbert Pinny in his office. He could be heard now, objecting: "*Mr. Hogg, a word if you please! Open this door at once!*"

The partygoers were all people Comity knew, and yet they were...altered. Did Quartz O'Malley Hogg have magic powers? Was his walking cane truly a sorceror's wand? Because suddenly Amos was...*not Amos*, and Hart was not Hart. Mr. Sankey could not stand upright without overbalancing and tottering sideways. Cage's seven sisters would not have recognized the rubber-legged, grinning fool trying and failing to put on his spectacles.

Comity stayed hidden. What to do? Watch. Bide her time. Wait for the right moment to step forward out of the shadows and call a halt.

But the moment never came.

"Caught him trying to break into the store," said Hogg. He seemed to think it hugely funny. "With a stolen lantern and wearing the Stationmaster's jacket, no less! We seem to be harbouring a thief in our midst."

And instantly the skinny boy they all knew by name, had all seen toiling in the garden and labouring at the forge bellows, was a thief, a criminal. The rubbery grins on their faces smeared into scowls.

A righteous gleam lit the eyes of Smith the smith. "Going to be sorry now, boy," he said and wrenched the jacket off Fred, as though skinning a rabbit. He bound Fred's hands behind his back with the thinner of his two belts.

Hogg expressed no rage. It seemed the greatest joke in the world that Fred should have turned up at the party uninvited. "Tell me, boy. Where is my charming young fiancée this evening? Speak up! You her pet dingo and not know her whereabouts? What use is a dog that cannot sniff out its owner?"

The men tittered and snorted…though Hogg's fancy sentences wound round their brains like ivy; they could not fully catch his drift.

"You know what, my excellent comrades? I have a mind to go dingo hunting. A piece of sport I have not seen since my days in the Army. You get a pest problem, you got to cull. You got to cull, or before you know it you are overrun. So who's for a little sport?"

There was a general enthusiasm; few could have said for what. Smith, though, being a man after Hogg's own heart, understood him completely. So, too, did the Aboriginal women, for they melted away: slipped out of the lamplight and vanished like woodsmoke, taking with them the figures among the trees.

"What are we doing?" asked Amos blearily, stumbling over an open can of whitewash left standing on the verandah.

"We are going hunting," said Smith with a smirk. "Hunting dingo."

"Remember to hang the carcass on the cat tree after," mumbled Sankey, who was slumping sleepily sideways in Comity's chair. "Keeps more vermin from coming."

A hoot of laughter burst from Hogg that was worthy of Loud Lulu. "Shall I do that, dingo? Shall I hang your carcass on the cat tree after, to scare off the rest of your kind? I believe I shall!" And pushing his face up close to Fred's, he painted a large white X on the boy's chest.

CHAPTER ELEVEN

The Hunt

He painted another X on Fred's back.

"No camouflage tonight, jacky. Got to give a chap an even chance, eh? Got to be sporting. You in sporting mood tonight, jacky? You got the legs on you for a good run?"

Some of the partygoers began to frown, others to snigger.

"*Mr. Hogg! Open this door at once! What is going on? I demand an explanation!*"

Quartz Hogg ignored the Stationmaster as he had done for weeks. To him, Herbert Pinny was a harmless rodent squeaking in the wainscot. "Saddle the horses, Mr. Hart," he said.

Hart took several steps backwards along the verandah. "I just have to fetch a…some…thing. Give me a while. I've had a drop too much…" Then he turned and bolted for the barn.

Comity was too slow to dodge out of sight. Hart saw her, plain as plain. But in his muddled, befuddled state, the oddness of her standing there, in the shadow of the barn, at three in the morning, seemed not to strike him. "Too far," he told her. "This has gone too far." Then he broke into a galumphing run and climbed the ladder to his room in the roof.

Amos did Hogg's bidding instead of Hart. He headed for the barn to saddle horses, but spotting Starbuck and the trap standing conveniently to hand, he blinked a few times in surprise then called back towards the house. "Buggy's ready and waiting!"

Without the jacket and with hands tied behind his back, Fred's skinny shoulders seemed narrower than ever; he was a matchstick figure – like the ones drawn on the pitch-and-toss stones scattered in the yard. Hogg got into the pony-trap with Smith, jovially inviting the others to saddle up and follow on behind.

But a blurry confusion thick as syrup had overtaken the

stockmen and the wiremen. Herbert Pinny's voice nagged them from the machine room. "*Let me out! Unbar this door! I demand you open…*"

"What are we doing?" Cage asked of Amos, and Amos shrugged and yawned and looked embarrassed.

As Smith hauled his huge bulk into the trap, Fred seized his chance. He took off and ran, heading for the paddock. Comity, who had slipped back inside the barn, watched him go through a knothole in the planks. Hogg gave a chortling laugh and took up his shotgun from the floor of the pony cart. He made great play of taking aim on the luminous white cross that danced among the trees. His finger tightened on the trigger.

Click. The gun was empty, the bullets safe in Fred's dillybag. By the time he had pulled out his army pistol, the painted cross on Fred's back was out of sight.

His happiness barely dented, Hogg took up the reins. Starbuck was startled into movement. Hogg drew out, from beneath the seat, a tin of cartridges and set Smith the task of loading. "The hunt is on, gentlemen. Follow my lead!" And away they went in the glare of the moon, the cart listing under the great weight of Smith.

But instead of following, the other men turned back into the house: dazed and hazed, perhaps they were looking for the party. Earlier there had been a party, that much they knew. Now all of a sudden there was nothing but a smell of spilled whitewash, and the Stationmaster's voice demanding to be let out of the machine room.

Instead of unjamming the door, instead of receiving an official reprimand and losing their jobs, they stayed sprawled along the verandah, nursing their drinks, desperately hoping the whole evening was a bad dream, a drunken imagining, nothing more. Perhaps if they drank still more, the memory of it might disappear altogether.

Despite Pinny's shouted demands to know what had been going on, no one shouted back with an explanation. No one told him what had just happened. So Pinny comforted himself that at least Comity was on her way to safety, with Fred for company. Trapped in the back room of Telegraph House, he had no way of knowing that Fred was just then running for his life across the pastureland, dodging between startled cattle.

Comity tried to lift a saddle onto Cage's horse, but the saddle weighed too much, and the horse kept moving away from her, unwilling to work again until morning. Hart's gelding kept its bristly lips tightly pursed against the bit. Only Amos's mare, biggest of the three, allowed Comity to put a bridle on her.

"Help me. Help me, Mr. Hart! We have to help Fred!" she called up at the loft, but no feet appeared over the edge of the loft hatch.

She had to stand on a straw bale to climb onto the horse's back, and then it insisted on visiting the manger for a bite of breakfast before deigning to stumble out into the moonlight. Comity ducked her head to avoid a hideous cobweb. Only then did she see that Hart had come to the loft hatch to watch her. The look on his face was unreadable – shame, apology and disgust, all stitched up inside a green headache.

"Why did you let him, Mr. Hart? Why did you not stop him?"

He shrugged. "'S'only a jacky," he said in a slurred whine, and she shut her heart against him, utterly, forever.

After she was gone, Hart headed back to the party, to try and ease the pain.

The trap tracks were easy to see in the moonlight, easy to follow. She would rather have followed Fred, but his bare feet left no trace discernible to any but the cleverest eye. That is why Hogg would never catch him. Never catch him. Fred would simply melt away into the night…

129

...hands tied behind his back, in a world squirming with snakes.

The horse showed no interest in trotting; without a saddle to cling to, Comity would probably have fallen off if it had. So they plodded along while, ahead of her, somewhere far out of sight, Quartz Hogg bowled along in the pony-trap probably doing that horrible whistling where he sucked instead of blew and did not bother with a tune. *If that is the worst noise he makes* (thought Comity, striking a mental deal with Jesus) *the whistling is fine. Just as long as there are no more gunshots.*

There again, without the gunshots, she would probably never have found them at all.

The sound came from over to her left and behind her; she must have missed seeing where the wheel-tracks had turned off the trail to wind between the great swirls of spinifex. Comity told herself it was the sound of a widow-maker shedding a bough. But when a second crack followed, and a third, she could not fool herself any longer.

Night was turning grey with anxiety. Morning was bullying it aside. Fred needed the darkness to hide him. Comity peered around, hoping to glimpse her friend, at the same time wishing him as invisible as Tuckonies.

She found that her days of roaming about with Fred had

taught her more than she'd realized: she actually knew where she was. Fred was moving in a circle, heading back now towards Miser's Creek and his railcar gunyah.

Had been. Had been heading for the railcar, until Hogg spotted him.

Quick-licking dawn uncovered the pony and trap. It had come to a halt on a sandy mound that raised it a little above the surrounding landscape. Smith was still seated, but Hogg had stood up, rifle to his shoulder, watching, patiently watching for any sign of movement. He knew his dingo had gone to ground – he had sighted the boy momentarily. He knew to be patient: the growing daylight would show him his prey.

He was concentrating so hard, watching for the smallest movement, that he was not aware of Comity at all until her horse's hoofs clacked together. He swung round, rifle and all, and Comity saw the round, black muzzle's end. She fully expected the hammer to fall, the flash, the stock to kick… Quartz Hogg looked at her along the barrel and smiled his babyish smile.

"Look, Smith. My fancy little fiancée wants to be in at the kill!" The syllables rolled and grated in his mouth like stones.

The thudding in Comity's ears grew louder. She thought it was her heartbeat until it took on material shape, bounding out of the half-light: a kangaroo. The Big Red thump-thump-thumped along with effortless grace, each bound spanning a prodigious space, then plucking up twin tufts of dust as the roo stamped its mark on the wilderness. *This place is mine*, it seemed to say. Its route towards Miser's Creek took it between the girl on the horse and the pony-trap.

Hogg's crystal buttons glinted as he turned. A single shot felled the kangaroo, which tumbled out of elegant flight into a jumble of joints, foot bones and ginger tail, with a loud grunt and a gusty sigh.

Smith had turned to watch the kangaroo die: both hunters' heads were facing away from Fred, who saw his chance. Crouched down behind a termite mound, he rose unsteadily to his feet now, no hands to help him and dizzy from sudden movement. A tingling raged through his cramped legs, but he ran, even so, hoping the diversion might give him the time he needed.

But Comity, in seeing him, must have sat up straighter, refocused her eyes, allowed her face to brighten, because Hogg turned to look where she was looking. Calmly he broke open his rifle, expelled the used cartridge, reloaded. He took aim on the running figure, on the white, painted cross almost luminous in the half-light of dawn.

Unlike the big red roo, Fred went down without a sound.

CHAPTER TWELVE

Heat and Cold

Starbuck, doubly startled, jinked forward in her traces and jerked the trap. Quartz Hogg sat down sharply. Comity slid off her horse and started to run the furlong to the buggy. She could not breathe: a roaring noise was emptying her lungs of air. As she ran, she stopped and picked up stones and began to throw them. She threw them with all her might, over and over again, rearming herself as she ran on. The stones began to hit the wheels, the tailgate, the upholstery. Smith, who had turned to watch Fred die, gave a startled grunt as a stone hit him in the neck. Another hit Starbuck, who towed the trap off the summit of the rise, and again the men lost their balance. Comity went on running, went on pelting them with stones. One caught Smith on the ear, one hit Hogg on the back of the head. What she would have done when she reached the trap, even she did not know. But chortling amusement gave way to curses, and having achieved his objective, Quartz Hogg recovered control of the cart and turned in a wide circle to head for home. He drove at Hart's horse to frighten it away: the long walk home would teach the girl a lesson.

It was the longest distance she had ever run, or so it felt. Past the dead kangaroo, past the termite mound, past the belt that had finally slipped from Fred's wrists; past the blood spatter... Her skirts hampered her, her boots weighed like lead, her hair got in front of her eyes and stopped her seeing.

"*Fred?*"

He was lying on his side in the dust, one arm flung up over his head, his legs bent as if he was still running, a pool of blood beneath him. But he lay so still that the flies were drinking sweat from his armpit undisturbed. His xylophone ribcage was perfectly silent and still. A few termites still clung to the hairs of his skin. She brushed them off – and felt the muscles flinch.

"They are gone," she said. "You can come out now," –

just as if he was under the verandah and she up top reading too scary a book.

The ribcage did swell then. The fingers did flex, but Fred did not sit up. Comity lay down so as to see under his arm, and his eyes were open, as if he was listening, ear-to-the-ground, deducing clever things about the coming and going of hoofs. "Fred?"

His eyes moved to focus, but drifted apart again into a blank stare. A tear crawled down the side of his nose. Fred was not feigning deadness; he was dying.

"We should go to your gunyah," she said.

His eyebrows signalled his dismay, his desire to be spared the effort. But Comity insisted. They could not go home, or Hogg would finish what he had started, and kill Fred for sure – Comity too, maybe, because she had seen him shoot down a child. And at least Fred's gunyah was close by. Besides, without a plan, she would have simply to sit back on her heels and howl like a dingo, and what good would that do? No one would come.

The mare came. Hogg's attempts to scare her away had turned the obstinate, idle nag into a nervy foal in need of comfort. She walked up behind Comity, reins dangling down from her mouth to trip her up, and swung her big head against Comity's back. *Do something. Do something,* the horse seemed to say.

So she did. Somehow she persuaded Fred to his feet, crawled between his legs and levered him off the ground astride her shoulders. He transferred his weight to the horse, and Comity looped the reins back over its head and put them into Fred's right hand. Without straw bale or stirrups she tried using the termite mound for a mounting block... But the mound crumbled under her and a hysteria of termites infested her legs and set her dancing: a dance fit to summon up an army of Tuckonies.

So she walked beside the horse's head, leading it towards Miser's Creek. It annoyed her that she could not remember what Amos called his mare. "I shall call you Horse," she said, so sharply that the mare tossed her head aside.

At any moment Comity expected Hogg to come back – to punish her for throwing stones, to return her to the station, to silence her tittle-tattle with a bullet.

She dared not look round at Fred. Cuts are all right. Sprains are easy if you have a bandage to hand. But holes in shoulders are not. Holes welling blood are distinctly... not. Fred's breathing was quick and shallow, snatched up every now and then by a jolt of pain as Horse lunged into a dip or stepped over brushwood.

Comity felt the risen sun begin to scorch her from behind. It was like being watched by a monstrous, blazing eye. Had the Kadimakara broken loose after Fred opened the storeroom door? Or did the Devil-Devil, punisher of wickedness, have her in its sights?

She had, after all, got her only friend shot.

Fred's railcar was a furnace. The metal was so hot it was painful to touch. The interior was a solid chunk of sweltering air. Comity climbed up and lowered herself through the carriage door, to fetch a pan from the sideways stove. By the time she hauled herself out again, she thought she could feel her internal organs cooking inside her like kidneys in a pie.

"You cannot go in there," she told Fred, who perfectly agreed. Instead they sat in the brook – or rather the small upwelling of sandy mud it had become since their last visit. Frogs struggled by, clarty with gouts of pink sand. Comity filled the pan as best she could and set it on the hot metal of the carriage, certain it would boil.

She had also fetched from the train the suitcase with Fred's treasures in it. She set the wire-rimmed spectacles on his nose, the celluloid collar on his labouring brown throat, the pipe in his hand. The umbrella she opened to shade them both from the sun.

Why could the cold black night and the sear white day not learn to share? Why did they cling to their differences?

Could they not exercise a bit of comity and share out the heat between them? Comity expressed this idea and several others to Fred as she tried to clean the hole in his shoulder. Fred said nothing at all.

She went to check on the water. It had not boiled. Was that important? Her mother always talked of boiling water as if it mattered, but perhaps that was only for cooking. Perhaps unboiled water tasted bad – which did not matter in the case of a hole. She asked Fred, but Fred only shrugged – started to shrug and then regretted it very much. It could definitely not be good for the flies to be crawling around the hole like that, sucking his blood through their long tongues. She gave Fred the flowery golden spike of a wichetty bush to keep the flies at bay.

At any moment she expected him to tell her what they should do. Unlike Moses in the Bible, who had wandered about lost for forty years, Fred could find his way around the wilderness. Fred was so much better than Moses.

"We do not want to go to ghantown," she suggested, and Fred shook his head in agreement. But Fred did not say what they should do instead. "We cannot go home, I mean, can we?" Comity suggested. Fred expressed no opinion either way, because he had fainted, falling squelchily backwards into the creek, disturbing a vast cloud of flies from the jellied weeds.

Comity considered tearing up her dress for bandages, but it was dirty with dust and caked in Horse's sweat. Besides, you have to keep yourself covered up in the sun if you are not Aboriginal or your skin falls off. So she took off her spencer instead and put her dress back on. The spencer was damp with sweat…but very well made and, try as she might, would not tear. Delving into Fred's dillybag in search of something sharp, she found six stones, a flint lighter, his wizened baby bandicoot, the shells from Hogg's rifle and some fine wire stolen from Jesus' gunyah.

"Thou shalt not steal," she told Fred sternly, because it was what her mother would have said. "I am most disappointed in you, Fred."

But it is hard to be disappointed in your only friend when his eyes are flickering under his lids and his ribcage is all twisted over in the mud. She went to get the kettle and tipped the gritty contents into the hole in Fred's shoulder, hoping he would not feel the heat, and glad it had not boiled after all.

"The Wire must be busy," she told Fred, "or Papa would have come looking."

But her father thought they were safe at Calgo Crossing and knew nothing of Fred's secret gunyah in any case. She could ride home – tell him – fetch help! And have Hogg call her a liar and lock her in her bedroom and stop her ever coming back…? No. Instead, Hogg would seek out the gunyah and…and it would all be Comity's fault.

When the day cooled, she managed to persuade Fred that the railcar would be a better place to spend the night. She bent her back for him to climb up onto the side of the capsized carriage. He tumbled inside like a coin into a money box, overturning the crate that served as his bookcase. Much-loved books Comity had mislaid and searched for high and low slithered across the floor.

"Thou shalt not take another person's books," said Comity helping Fred into one of the sideways-tilted wooden seats.

But it is hard to lecture your only friend when his limbs are jumpy with cold and he groans softly to himself and won't open his eyes. His head was against the window and she saw his hair quiver as a shudder ran through the whole railcar. Tethered to the railcar, Horse had begun to rub herself against the metalwork and to crib on the reins securing her. The rasp of her coarse hair against the carriage sounded as loud as a ripsaw.

As the carriage cooled, it clicked and pinged eerily. Comity shivered.

"Three dog night, verily." Fred's voice made her jump. "Feet to the fire. Dogs on top. Plenty big warm dogs. Like Gayfire Bobby."

She could almost have smacked him. Mama had read them the story of Greyfriars Bobby, and Greyfriars Bobby had *not* slept on top of his master to keep him warm on a raw wilderness night. Loyal Greyfriars Bobby had slept on top of his master's grave after he was…

"Greyfriars Bobby was not big. He was only little," she snapped. "And sleeping under dogs can give you fleas. I shall light the stove."

He did not protest. His teeth were chattering with cold.

She had his flint lighter. She had the kindling. Feeling about for one of the fallen books, she pulled the pages out one by one, crumpling them in her fist. Opening the stove, she pushed them loosely in. The paper would be gone in moments, but the bindings might burn for long enough to warm the carriage and boil some drinking water. Comity flicked the wheel of the flint lighter and brought its flame up close to the paper… How scared it must be, that flame; see how violently it quivered in her hand.

A paper ball or two dropped out of the stove in front of her. The snake that had made its nest in the stove pushed its head out through the bank of crumpled paper and looked at her, eyes reflecting the lighted flame, tongue tasting the fear in the air. Comity slammed the oven door with a clang.

"Too big noise," said Fred, his eyes opening wide with terror. He had begun to see Hogg's face in every smear of moonlight on the dirty windows.

How many other snakes were coiled up in the luggage nets or under the floor or amid the broken clutter of the wrecked carriage? What fruity spiders? What scorpions? What Tuckonies? What ghost camels, what ghosts of those killed in the train crash? Comity climbed onto the backrest of an upended seat opposite Fred, drew her knees up to her chest and sat in a tight, shuddering ball. The image of the snake stayed bright in her mind's eye. Other monsters began to edge their way in as well.

"Fred. Hey, Fred," she asked at some point during the night. "What did it look like, the Kadimakara? You saw inside the store. You must have seen."

"I seen in," said Fred.

"And?"

"Not. Nothing," he said. "No Kadimakara." And he set his mouth in that way that meant, *I was not wrong: someone just changed the truth.*

Like a conjuror's assistant, she stayed curled up while night drove blades of cold through and through and through the box in which she and Fred lay hiding. Above their heads, above the carriage door which constituted a skylight, shooting stars went over like bullets.

"Tomorrow someone will come," she said doubtfully. "Someone who is not Mr. Hogg."

Horse twanged her rope and scratched her haunches against the train, fearing dingoes.

Towards morning, Fred stopped feeling the cold. Fever had crept in at the hole in his shoulder.

At the crack of dawn, Comity stood up on her seat and pushed the carriage door upwards.

CRACK.

On the first gust of fresh air came a crack so loud that she let the door drop.

CRACK CRACK.

Gunfire.

Her hearing dimmed as fear shut off the blood supply. Her mouth, already parched with thirst, ran drier still.

If it was Hogg out there, there was nothing to stop him strolling right up to the train, climbing up on its side, looking down at her through the windows and taking a slow, deliberate aim. But maybe it was not Hogg at all, but a dozen murderous ghans intent on doing all those things Hogg had described across the dinner table; all those hideous, unthinkable, unforgettable things…

"We going?" enquired Fred, coughing up the words like phlegm.

"Not yet," said Comity, climbing down. "Later, maybe. Does that suit, Mr. Fred?"

"Byallmean, Mrs. Pinny," said Fred.

CRACK CRACK. Again the rifle shot. Had they shot Horse? (There was no more twanging of rope or scratching of hide against metal.) But no thud shook the carriage. No bullet penetrated the roof or floor or broke the windows. Ten minutes, an hour passed, peppered by the occasional CRACK of a rifle.

Were Comity and Fred meant to surrender? Did the ambusher think they were armed? Or were they simply keeping their victims pinned down, and waiting for Fred to die? It was true: time was not on Fred's side.

Comity gathered to her everything she might use to defend herself. It did not amount to much: a dinner knife, knitting needles, a porcelain spearhead. (Boiling water would have been good if she could have lit the stove.) Another hour passed, crazed with the crack of gunfire. Still nothing hit the railcar – only the sun slamming into the metalwork, heating the space inside to cooking temperature.

What if it was just someone hunting nearby? Someone not Quartz Hogg. What if it was just someone from

Kinkindele killing pestiferous dingoes and cats or teaching himself to shoot straight? What if there was help at hand, and Comity was sitting under a railcar seat, clutching a pair of knitting needles while Fred's sweat dripped on her through the slats?

"I think I shall go and take a look," she said, touching his coarse wiry hair. His eyes rolled as they opened.

Comity climbed up and pushed at the carriage door. Her arms felt feeble, unequal to hauling her up and out. And what if, when her head emerged…

CRACK!

Comity tumbled back down and burst into tears.

"They are shooting at us, Fred!"

"Yes?" He cocked his head slightly and listened. He did not have to wait long.

CRACK.

"No."

"What do you mean, no? Listen!"

CRACK.

Fred said, "Rifle bird."

Half a day wasted. Comity was in a towering rage – with herself, with the rifle bird, with Jesus for playing silly jokes at a time when jokes were not appropriate – not appropriate in the least! Now they must travel through the heat of the day. Now she was so much more weary when it came to Fred standing on her shoulders to escape the railcar; also when it came to getting out herself. She kept her temper fuelled – *stupid rifle bird…stupid invention… why should a bird need to make a noise like a rifle?* – because temper is a kind of energy…and sometimes you can squash fear with it, like you can squash beetles with a rock.

Temper helped Comity to get them both up onto Horse's back. (Horse was not, of course, lying dead on the ground riddled with bullet holes, but had broken loose to drink from the gloopy dregs of the creek.) If only temper made a person clever, then Comity might have known where to go.

"Ghantown?" she said doubtfully.

"No," said Fred, and a wave of gratitude went through Comity. Fred was back on form. Now she need not go to the tintown and she need not be the person who decided.

"You know somewhere? Somewhere with people?"

"Verily," said Fred, his hands sunk in his dillybag, fingering the six smooth pebbles he kept there. "Time to go in Altjeringa. You want to go along me." It was not a question but a statement. "You want to go in Altjeringa."

"Where?" His speech was not very clear any more, and

was further confused by a whistling, rasping sound in his throat. "Go where, Fred? Very good, but where?"

"Trail of Yooneerara. To Byamee's gunyah."

It was nothing but a string of vowels stitched together with spit. Comity's temper bubbled up again. "Speak clearly please, Mr. Fred. I cannot understand you."

"Time to die, lilly-pilly. Got to get to Altjeringa. Like Yooneerara did on his two feet. Byamee is pretty damn old. Reckon I have to shout in his ear: *Fred is coming, kubang. You got a space ready by the fire?*" He broke off to cough, his forehead resting on Horse's mane. His spine was so bent that Comity could see the shape of every vertebra: like porcelain insulators strung along the Wire.

"All right, Fred," said Comity sternly, pretending she had been asked and not told. "Altjeringa. But not forever. We go. You get healed. We come back again. Like Yoonywhoeversomebody. Or how would *I* get home?"

CHAPTER THIRTEEN

On the Way to Altjeringa

Horse (being the property of the British-Australian Telegraph Company) was accustomed to following the Wire. During tours of inspection, for weeks at a time, she would plod along the shadowline of the overhead cable. Without the Wire, Horse was inclined to stand still. Comity's legs grew weary from kicking her in the flanks. Little blisters were starting to rise on her forearms and the backs of her hands. Small wonder Fred's ancestors had turned themselves into rocks and hills and trees: out here, when the sun got to work, flesh-and-blood was not a good thing for a person to be.

Horse was not enjoying herself either. *That boy is dying.*

"He is not," said Comity. "We are on a quest."

Since Station Four had been built bang on top of the traditional Kinkindele burial grounds, funerals no longer took place there. But Fred did not much care where his body was buried: it was his spirit he was worried about. Would the songlines within the landscape tell his soul the right way to go? Would they give him the energy, too, to press on and get there? Because his ancestors *were* the landscape – that tree, that rock, that bandicoot – and his ancestors possessed all the magic healing he needed to reach…

To reach what?

The far side of death? His mother? Some resting place between lives past and lives in the future? If Fred could have grown to manhood, and been initiated into the mysteries, he might have known more things for certain.

He began to sing. It was more of a murmur – barely halfway to a hum – but a song is a measure of distance travelled and he knew he must keep track of how far they had come.

"Why? How far is it to Altjeringa?" asked Comity.

"Need plenty songs," said Fred, who had no idea.

When the singing fell silent, Comity began asking questions. If she could think of one question every mile, maybe she could keep Fred's spirit from sliding out of his body.

"Why is your ma not here any more?"

"She went up to visit her mob. Never come there. Never come back. No sign."

Comity knew there were any number of reasons why a person might walk off into the rising sun and never be seen again: an illness, a snake, bad water, wild dogs...
"Your pa must have been sad. But at least he still has you!"

"No father, me. Like Jesus, me."

"What, you mean an angel gave your ma the good news?"

"Nah. My old woman need no man. She standed under coolibah tree. Best way."

Once again, Comity could only wonder at the magic of the Outback, where ancestors petrified into rocks, and trees shed magic onto women and made them pregnant. "That is wonderful, Fred. That is what I shall do, if ever I want a baby."

"Only way. One and alonely way."

"Fred. Wake up, Fred. In the story; why did Curlew curse Mopoke so he could never go outside?" Comity had finally found a rockpile and managed to climb astride Horse.

"Mopoke kill all Curlew chicks."

"Well there you are, then! Papa never killed *anyone*. He cannot be curlew-cursed, can he?"

"Fred, listen. Listen, Fred. How old are you?"

But Fred did not know. "Oldest I ever gonna be," he said, and sobbed. Comity did not know whether it was from pain or regret at all the birthdays he would never live to see.

"Fred. Fred, listen. Why—?"

Fred dropped his forehead against her back and sighed. "Less talk," he said.

"More talk," said Comity ruthlessly. If Fred stopped talking, then his soul might slip from the horse when she was not looking.

But this time it was Fred who asked the question. "You gonna venge me, lilly-pilly? Make boots?"

"'Venge you? On Mr. Hogg? Of course I will. I promise. I will make boots, Fred, I promise." She even knew the recipe; they had talked about it while Fred ground pituri leaves between two spoons and Comity made lemonade. Take emu feathers and the blood of a whole emu and stick the feathers together into boots. The boots would help you hunt down your enemy. "I will follow him and follow him.

He will never escape me. I will do a revenge for you, Fred, I promise on my honour."

"Drink be good, Mrs. Pinny," said Fred, who had begun to confuse Comity with her mother.

Syrupy with weariness and slick with sweat, Comity easily slid into the role. "When we find water, we shall light a fire and find those eggs parrots lay in the spinifex... and form a *plan*. A plan is most important, Fred."

But Fred already had a plan, didn't he? He was planning to follow in the footsteps of his mythic hero Yooneerara, all the way to the home of the Creator of the World.

"Fred. Fred, sorry to disturb, but what should *I* do when we get to Altjeringa?" she asked. She knew it sounded selfish and bleating and she was ashamed to mention it. There again, it *was* a question, and she had to keep the questions coming.

A flicker of the old Fred surfaced. He gave the question what thought he could spare. "You go to ghantown," he said.

"*What?*"

"Ghans like fat womans. Everybody says."

Comity was horrified and bewildered. "But, Fred, I'm *not* fat!"

"So? You be safe there."

It made no sense at all to Comity. She lapsed into silence, imagining herself in the hands of murderous heathens who hated her because she was not fat.

"Too far," said Fred suddenly. Comity had thought him asleep, but Fred had been checking his non-existent map, and the distance to Altjeringa had overwhelmed him. Maybe a thousand, maybe a thousand thousand songs lay between him and Altjeringa. Drawing breath enough for one song was hard, what with the hole in his shoulder and Horse's jarring gait.

"Altjeringa is not so very excellent," he said in a voice intended to sound scornful. "Let us rise and go even unto the Land of the Moon. That's verily a bang-on place."

"Sounds nice," said Comity, trying to keep the panic out of her voice. "Is it far?"

She was relieved to hear that the Land of the Moon lay just over the horizon – relieved to be spared the trek to somewhere that did not exist, even if it meant going somewhere else that probably did not exist either. It was a wonder more people did not go to the Land of the Moon, because apparently it was beautiful, with grassy hills and valleys watered by streams and strewn with flowers where

Moon Bahloo dipped low to kiss his children goodnight before setting off across the sky. "Bahloo is fine, jolly chap," said Fred. "He take me along with him, eh? Not let his dogs eat me? He got two damn big dogs."

"He will say, 'Suffer little Fred to come unto me'," said Comity. "Then he will let down a rope and say, 'Come aboard thou good and faithful fellah'."

But part of her wanted to cry. Not because she did not believe in the Land of the Bahloo, but because her friend, the fearless, resolute, decided Fred, had given up on Byamee-the-Beginner-of-all-Things-and-Time, and settled for the moon instead.

Thought you were a Christian, said Horse, her bony spine sagging. *Moon Bahloo indeed. He's not in the Bible.*

"It is what Fred believes that matters. Not what I believe," she told the horse. And, for the first time, she wondered if this was true. Should she not break it to Fred that he was a pagan – a nice pagan, but a pagan? What if his soul jumped up to the moon, and it turned out to be just a lump of rock, and he had to come down again? Fred hated to be made to look stupid.

We're all going to die of thirst out here, observed Horse dismally.

"Not while there are zebra finches!" said Comity, and straightened her own backbone. For flying across her vision – in ones and two, then in fives and tens – was a dizzy flicker of black-and-white birds.

And zebra finches are a sure sign of water.

Within ten minutes, Horse scented water herself. She broke into a trot that pulled the reins out of Comity's blistered hands. Then the ground itself began blistering into mounds and hummocks that were the colour of bruises. A hundred steps more and the landscape broke out in a rash of flowers and mulga thickets. Beside shallow pools made turquoise by a host of budgerigars, white-backed swallows had built their mud nests overhanging the water. There were squat trees with corellas bobbing among their branches. As a change from the flies that had peppered every step of the way, there were dragonflies now, and bees.

The difference was so marked in Fred that Comity knew he mistook this place for the Land of the Moon. His spirit was dancing, expectant of some great magic.

"If you are going to leap up to the moon, you must eat a good supper first," said Comity bossily. "We shall wash your hands and then I shall cook dinner." It did not matter what she said, Fred's attention was somewhere else.

Cook supper? First she had to find some.

A black duck took one look at her and flew away. The parrots hereabouts did not lay their eggs on the ground.

She knew Fred would dig for frogs, but how do you kill a frog, even if you manage to catch one? Or force fat white grubs between your lips and chew on them and swallow them down your throat?

That boy is dying, said a bush turkey, strutting by.

"But he might get well if I cook you and give him food."

You can try! said the turkey, and ran off, as laughing and shrill as Loud Lulu.

She watched a butcher bird bring down a pretty little pipit and impale it on a twig, then break into cheerful song, tilting its head this way and that, choosing just where it would stick in its beak and rip open the pipit. "Die, Mr. Hogg!" said Comity and threw a rock at the butcher bird. Miles wide.

The goanna was a mistake, plain and simple. She saw a movement in the corner of her eye, threw a rock, and killed the lizard stone dead by accident.

She gathered a fistful of seeds, but it felt like tipping a handful of grit into Fred's mouth.

"*Koppi unga*," said Fred. What did it mean? What did he need her to do?

"Food for Fred be nice, Jesus," said Comity. "I know he's not a Christian quite, but you have to be nice to people

156

different from you and forgive them if sometimes they steal things…" And that got her thinking about the stationery store and porcelain insulators and fine wire…

…which was how she came to make a fish-hook-and-line out of stolen wire, and catch three fish. Piling grass and twigs around them, she set it all aflame with the flint lighter. She threw the lizard on the fire too, but not to eat. "Good on you, Jesus, sir," she said, and was momentarily ready to overlook the business of the tiger snake. They ate the fish skewered on her ancestral knitting needles.

In the end, though, the goanna made Fred happier than any food.

On the side the bullet had entered, his neck muscles had grown rigid and he could not turn his head, but his hands groped blindly for his dillybag. Spilling it on the ground, he felt about for the contents, and suddenly Comity remembered him talking about some ancestor who had rubbed six stones with lizard fat…

"*Kurlang*," he said, mouth rigid and pulled out of shape by the muscles in his neck. "*Djanak kurlang! Kert-kert*." Seeing her blankness, he made a titanic effort to muster English words; it was like digging for frogs. "Sons! I want sons, lilly-pilly! To remember Fred!" Tears ran down the creases of his face.

Somewhere during the ride, or in getting down from

Horse, the dillybag must have torn a little. The cartridge cases and five of the stones were gone; only one smooth pebble lay beside the shrivelled bandicoot baby and the remains of the stolen wire. Comity did not tell Fred this. Keeping to his blind side, she allowed him to see her rubbing that single stone over the greasy skin of the burned goanna until it was almost too slippery to grip. As Fred's ancestor did in the Dreamtime.

Comity closed her eyes and allowed sweet, golden imaginings to rise into her head like honey ants. And sure enough, she saw six stones hatch like eggs. Out of them came wisps of smoke – no, not smoke, but muscles and sinews and hanks of hair; faces and features.

"One of your sons has a shield, Fred, can you see? And one has a digging stick, and one has a woomera and one has a dog and one has a book."

One was dressed in tree bark, one in a patchwork waistcoat, one a skin cloak, one in body paint and two in long coats of purple velvet.

One was good at hunting, one singing, one telling stories and the fourth could speak to the animals. One knew the Morse Code, and the last…

"…can fly!" exclaimed Comity delightedly.

And to her genuine and total surprise, all of Fred's sons were…crying. They turned their faces away (because men hate to be seen crying), then they walked around behind her, into a part of her mind where she could no longer see them.

"They are all very handsome – like you," she told Fred. "And they say they will take you up to the moon."

"They speak?"

"No. But I understood. And if, when you get there, the moon is only rock, they will take you to Altjeringa instead."

Fred's eyes focussed on her for the first time in a day. They were lively with light and admiration. "I saw nothing, lilly-pilly. *Bulyakarak,* you are, *kubang. Bulyakarak.*" It sounded like a good thing to be.

An hour later, though, as the sun sank, Fred too must have caught sight of his sons, because he began to talk to them in a breathy whisper.

"*Allinger yerra-bamalla…mantanekin! Kulpernatoma! Yarrura? Windana? …Korr!*"

He seemed to be settling, subsiding like a house built on sand, like a verandah undermined by termites. He was troubled, too, by monsters he said were dogging their trail.

"You said yourself, dear. There was nothing in the stationery store," said Comity sternly. But Fred's head was crammed with monsters, his eyes empty of daylight.

"*Arcoona, arcoona! Windana, Comity? Wayarn, Comity. Wija narani, Comity!*"

Closer and closer she leaned, as if closeness might lend meaning to the garbled words. She pressed her ear to his chest, as if his heartbeat might speak to her in Morse, but all she heard was a bubbling racket…

…and then the whistling scream.

Fred had opened his eyes and was staring past her at a Dreamtime monster. "*Kadimakara! Thrunkkun! Go way! Thrunkkun!*"

Then she saw it too – saw the reflection of it in Fred's red-rimmed eyes. It was not imagined: it was all too real. And it was towering over them, ready to strike.

CHAPTER FOURTEEN

Feral

The camel came down on them, spitting and snorting, lips drawn back, jaws clacking together. It missed Comity's arm but its teeth closed on her dress and it pulled her clear of the ground and shook her violently, then let go. Before she had even touched the ground, the huge head struck her in the chest and flung her through the air to land on her back.

It knocked all the wind out of her. She would never draw breath again, she was sure – never have time to draw breath. The camel skidded on the spongy ground and turned – all kneecaps and filthy wool shag, its flaccid hump slumping to and fro. It realigned itself to stamp on her. Its back hoofs spread, its front ankles cracked together as it reared up. Its conjoined front hoofs took aim on her stomach, sharp and heavy as mattocks. Comity rolled aside until she collided with a rock. The hoofs sank into moss, and water droplets flew in every direction, turning to rainbows in the low light.

She was vaguely aware of a second camel – a figure – a turban – a whip – and thought how everything Hogg had said about the ghans was true. The camel recovered its footing and reared up a third time. There was nowhere left for Comity to roll, and she had not even the breath to scream.

With a thud that filled the air with dust and flies and tufts of wool, the camel's silhouette suddenly shared the sky with another just as large. A hoof trod on her thigh. A frog squirmed past her face. The grunting was so loud, the hoofs so many, that she thought she was being trampled by a whole herd of camels. Her attacker crashed down on its side, legs flailing, stretching its neck, breath rasping, shrieking dementedly, rolling to and fro until it was able to roll back onto its knees. Scrambling to its feet, it uttered a belching curse and staggered away at an ungainly trot.

The second camel watched it go, head erect in haughty contempt. Its rider cracked a whip at the departing beast, before sliding down to stand over Comity. His shape blotted out the declining sun so that he appeared to glow white-hot. Then he took off his turban and drew a knife.

"Are you very much hurt, please? These wild ones are a bane. A big bane," said the youth. "Their ancestors worked the goldfields, maybe. Some ran off into the Bush. Now there are wild camels all over."

He began to bandage her thigh with strips of his turban. "Low class stock, of course. The Australian camel is all-round better. We breed the best with the best. We get good camels. Good Australian camels."

Comity pointed and pointed, still mute for want of breath, mouthing, "Fred, not me! Fred!" And he searched out Fred, and Comity thought, *Now he will cut Fred's throat and it will be my fault because I told him Fred was there.*

When he came back, he blew life back into the fire Comity had lit earlier.

She knew him. Comity had always supposed all ghans looked alike and that she would never be able to tell them apart. But she did recognize the boy who came with the camel trains to Kinkindele; the one who did not look away when she took receipt of deliveries. He had come with the piano.

And he had not cut Fred's throat at all. He had covered the wound with a wad of white cloth, and bound it into place. He had felt Fred's thin wrist between finger and thumb and felt the flutter of his blood creeping about the passageways of his dusty body. But he did not answer when Comity asked, "Will Fred be all right?"

His name was Moosa Rasul. Quartz Hogg had said all ghans were called Mullah. Fred said they were all called "whitefellah-with-string-hair". But confusingly this one's name was Moosa Rasul, son of Salaiman, and he lived in the ghantown at Calgo Crossing. This and his mastery of English and his extraordinarily clean clothes startled Comity's terror into hiding. Considering how unfat she was, Moosa seemed remarkably friendly.

He came to the mound springs, he said, to read the Koran and to think up poetry in his head. He was probably lying and would torture and mutilate and massacre her and Fred later, when he had more light to see by. But in the meantime she was too tired to do anything but listen to his plans for breeding the finest camels in Australia. He recited one of his poems to her too, and his voice bobbed up and down pleasantly, like a budgerigar in a tree, but the poem was not in English, of course, so she could not understand it.

"Is that Ghan?" she asked.

"Punjabi," he said. "One thinks we come from Afghanistan but this is most largely untrue. Most in Calgo are from India. The Punjab. Me, however, I was born in Australia. I am Australian."

"Like the good camels."

He smiled broadly. Even his teeth seemed to be spotlessly clean. "Like the best camels." Behind them, his good Australian camel slumped to the ground like a ship foundering. Moosa leaped up instantly and ran to the saddle pannier and drew out a parcel wrapped in silk, and tucked it into the highest crook he could reach of a nearby tea tree – as though rescuing something precious from a flood. "High up. Always," he said shyly.

At sunset he washed in the spring pool and Comity heard him say prayers to his heathen god. Meanwhile, Fred, barely conscious, his head in Comity's lap, waited for a late moon to rise so that he might hurl his soul into Bahloo's arms for evermore. Comity said the Lord's Prayer, put in a word with Jesus for her mother and father, and hoped that, despite what people said about Him, God secretly believed in the comity of nations. Horse wandered off to the far side of the springs to be out of sight of the camel. Horses hate camels, and to judge by the look on the camel's ugly face, the feeling was mutual. Who did they say their prayers to? Comity wondered.

When the night grew bitter, Moosa took the saddle blanket from his all-Australian camel and laid it over Fred and Comity, then curled up alongside his animal for warmth. He had not planned to spend the night away from home, but his patients would not withstand travelling in the cold – not on top of sunburn, shock and injury. He woke them before moonset, though, shortly before dawn.

"Come. The day will be warm soon."

Comity *tried* to tell Moosa that Fred wanted to die here, at the mound springs, so that his soul might jump up to the moon, but Moosa seemed to have no respect for Fred's wishes.

"Would he not prefer to stay alive?" he asked, and went on constructing a travois by poking branches through the sleeves of his robe and lashing this hammock to the crupper of his camel's saddle.

"You can save him?"

"Allah is merciful."

What kind of answer was that? "Where are we going?" asked Comity.

"To my humble home, naturally," he said. "You must not deny me that honour."

Fred made a feeble attempt to escape – "*Yirra! Yirra!*" – but Moosa overruled him: "*Nah, kubang. Malka karak.*" He saw Comity's astonishment. "We should all learn to understand our neighbours." He laughed. "But it is madly impossible. I have maybe one hundred native words, and my father would like to sweep *those* out of doors. "'*Why speak to the jackies? They are not like us*'." That is his argument. '*Never mix the salt and the sand*.' A favourite saying here. But I say, mix it! Mix it up! The sea does, so why not us?"

Calgo Crossing was not, like Oodna, on either the railway or the Wire. It stood in barren wilderness, at the point where two camel routes crossed, beside a spring. Ninety miles to the south-east lay Oodnadatta; sixty miles to the north-east Kinkindele. A railway spur had been built a few years before, branching off the Oodna mainline, so as to deliver goods and mail direct to the cameleers in Calgo. But it was closed so often by flash flooding or sandstorms that it had fallen out of use.

The first sign Comity saw of the town was a carpet of fleshy, purple blossoms, finding water where none seemed to exist. The next was a row of half-buried houses. The branch-tips of two date trees reached up out of the dirt as well, like fingers scrabbling after air. Engulfed by a sandstorm, the first Calgo Crossing had been abandoned and then begun again farther on.

Next came an ancient camel turning a wheel to raise water from underground. The water flowed into stone troughs surrounded by orchards of oranges, mango trees and date palms, and garden beds full of garlic. Some of the houses were mud-built, some used galvanized sheets of iron. The mosque was bigger even than Telegraph House, its iron roof covered over with cane grass. And behind the tin mosque lay a cemetery where dozens of iron bedsteads stood in neat lines. Perhaps the ghans laid out their dead for the buzzards to eat, then let the bones just rattle through into the dust. Or perhaps not.

Comity had no idea if she was a prisoner or a hunting trophy brought home by Moosa. True, she had survived the night, but for all she knew that was because the ghans liked their meat fresh and she was the main ingredient for dinner. Calgo Crossing smelled of curried children, or so it seemed to Comity.

The women sitting by their doorways sewing, the children outside the schoolhouse, all watched Moosa's camel go by – then the travois containing the wreck of a boy, and then Comity riding Horse. Small children ran alongside. The men followed at a distance, drawn by curiosity and the chance to tell Moosa Rasul he was a fool.

So here they were, among people Fred hated and feared, and it was all Comity's fault, because she had not wanted Fred to die. Now he would be buried somewhere away from both his ancestors and the moon, and his soul would be left wandering far from home. She wanted to tell the police that Quartz Hogg had shot Fred in cold blood, but there were no policemen in Calgo: the ghans probably did not believe in laws.

The whole length of the single street, not one smile greeted them. Old men with faces like wrinkled leather scowled at Moosa and rapped at their heads as if the boy might have overlooked his turban or sacrilegiously thrown it away. But Moosa had used his turban to bandage Fred's wound and Comity's leg.

Moosa's parents were not overjoyed by the caravanserai of oddities he had collected. *Why? What made you bring these home?* said the faces in the living room. His father took off his spectacles so as to see less clearly Comity in her torn clothes. His wife fetched out a pristine white robe as big as a sail and engulfed Comity in it, along with a perfume of lemons. A girl brought her a tin cup of water; she was wearing clothes stitched with sequins and dyed sea-blue. The crowd gathering outside stared in at the door with open curiosity, and barely stepped aside as Moosa carried Fred indoors, dropping words in his face from between those supremely white teeth: "*Cull-la. Cull-la, kardang.*" Another child hardly taller than Comity's waist took hold of her hand, shaped it into a curve and deposited a warm sticky dollop of something into the palm.

Before long, the local doctor pushed his way through and began to undo all Moosa's careful bandaging. He seemed offended by the sight of an Aboriginal bleeding onto a Muslim mattress, and Moosa's mother instantly despatched the soiled turban for burning.

"Will he die? Will Fred be all right?" Comity asked, but the doctor spoke no English and no one chose to translate the question.

The air round Comity's head swarmed with the words of a mysterious language no Morse could ever transmit. She stared at their mouths, trying to understand, but had to fall back on guesswork. She guessed they were saying that Fred was dead but not worth eating.

Oh yes, and all this while she wept – helplessly, uselessly, ceaselessly, silently – her whole frame shaking and swaying like a tree in a sandstorm. The words, the sounds, the voices were burying her like those date trees, right up to the tips of her branches, until she could no longer breathe.

Somewhere outside, a thin, wavering voice rang out, and the crowd dispersed. Abruptly men and boys – including Moosa and the doctor – left to pray. The women too disappeared, and Comity was left entirely alone, thinking they must have gone to discuss what should be done with her. Perhaps she would be held captive, like

Rapunzel, in a tin tower, so that she would slowly roast. And her father would not come looking for her, because he was curlew-cursed. And Fred would not come and rescue her, because Fred would be lying dead on an iron bedstead in the cemetery, being eaten by buzzards.

She went and sat beside him. "I will make boots, Fred," she told him. "I will do like you said with the emu feathers and hunt him down. Hogg cannot hide from the emu boots, can he, Fred? I will. I promise."

Over dinner, Moosa explained his other plans for becoming successful. Not only were he and his father going to breed the best camels in Australia, they were also going to move into the production of toothbrushes made in the Punjabi way, from twigs frayed at one end.

"Cheap, very cheap. There is only labour to pay for, and it is work that women can do."

He wanted to expand the production of dates by planting more palms – a forest of date palms – and ship crate-loads from Oodnadatta to Adelaide and Melbourne. Also mango jam. Moosa had plans to sweeten every breakfast table in Australia with mango jam. Leaning forward to scoop up a mouthful of curry with finger and thumb, he would look eagerly across at Comity and the food would remain (in his hand) uneaten in mid-air while he propounded yet another business plan. It was almost as if he was defying her to blink, defying her to think. He asked her nothing about herself.

His father wanted to know what had happened at the mound springs. He even asked it in English.

"Attack by a wild camel," said Moosa with casual haste.

"But the jacky is shooted!"

"I saw nothing of that." Moosa simply would not let the conversation take Comity back to the horrors of the previous two days. He pinned her in the present moment with his intense, immense eyes and his lively conversation. "Of course, I wish above all to be a poet, but poetry is a gift from Allah. Baba – recite to Miss Comity 'The Lamp of God'. This is my father's favourite poem. Please be so good as to listen." And his eyes commanded her attention, coaxing her away from her own thoughts, packing her head with words as he had packed the wound in Fred's shoulder.

After the poem, his mother asked another question, which Moosa was happy to translate. "My mother asks what you think of our town."

Comity looked around her. Above every door in the house rested a silk-wrapped package like the one Moosa had wedged in the gum tree. *Up high. Always high.* She had tasted dates for the first time in her life and they were delicious. Beneath her, a threadbare carpet showed horsemen and fruit trees and peacocks. Outside, someone was singing a song from another continent.

"I think I want to go home," she said. "With Fred."

But next morning, when Comity woke, the mattress where Fred had lain was empty. The littlest girl brought Comity her clothes, washed and tied into a bundle; also a little packet of sweets.

"Where is Fred?" Comity asked, but the girl did not speak English.

An older girl brought her milk and dates, grapes and an orange and signalled her to dress in the robes she had been given the day before. Comity sensed an eagerness to have her out of the house. But first the girl made Comity pass three times through the door of the sleeping room, pointing to the silk-wrapped parcel over the lintel.

"Where is Fred?" Comity asked of Moosa's mother, who smiled encouragement but did not understand.

No tin prison tower awaited her outside. Only Moosa and Horse and sunshine as harsh as bleach. "Where is Fred?" she asked.

Moosa looked away. "Baba has sent a gift of sweets to

all the children in town," he said, and went to fetch his camel.

"Fred is dead?" she whispered to the world at large. Horse nodded her head up and down.

A wedge-tailed eagle flew over, higher than the rising sun, higher surely than the moon. She thought its beak must have scooped out her heart while she slept.

CHAPTER FIFTEEN

Hospitality

One person in Calgo *was* called Mullah, and that was the mullah who led prayers at the mosque. He thought it dangerous to have a lost British child in the town. *Never mix the salt and the sand:* a popular saying among the ghans. Also, a dog had been howling in the night, which was a bad omen. So Comity was being returned to Kinkindele as quickly as possible, like a misdirected parcel.

Though the journey was long enough to sing a hundred songs and ask just as many questions, Comity did neither. Horses hate camels and camels hate horses, so that Horse lagged way behind Mustapha the camel. (The saying must have been popular among horses and camels as well: *Never mix the salt and the sand.*) The distance between their mounts meant it was almost impossible for Moosa and Comity to talk.

She ate the sweets she had been given. The sweetness was a shock on her tongue. She had forgotten about sweetness. For a long time, there had been no sugar at Telegraph House. Hogg had said it fetched in ants, and had taken it away to the stationery store. It might have fetched in cakes too, thought Comity, and cakes might have fetched in happiness. Fred would have liked there to be cakes.

Comity watched Moosa, in his embroidered waistcoat and fresh white turban, sway to the movement of his all-Australian camel. She had forgotten about sweetness. She had forgotten – how had she managed to forget? – all the kindness of the previous day: the curry, the water, the bandages round her thigh where the camel had trodden on her, the bed conjured from nowhere, the poetry, the toothbrush given her to use and to keep, the fruit, the smiles, the fear pushed out of sight, the neighbours leading Horse off to the water troughs and bringing her back brushed and fed and with a sheepskin on her back, red threads plaited into her mane. How had Comity forgotten the little silk-wrapped parcels balanced above every doorway, that blessed her each time she passed below them and would keep her safe on her journey? How had she forgotten the billowing yards of cloth swathing her sunburned skin in softness, the arms round her, soothing her sorrow? Not her father's, but Punjabi arms.

When they camped at noon, Moosa rigged a canopy of cloth stretching from the saddle of his kneeling camel to a row of securing rocks, so that Comity could rest in the shade. He himself sat at a distance, cross-legged in the sun, until the sun told him it was time to pray.

"You are like a good Samaritan," she said as he kneeled and let her use his back for a mounting block. "You helped us."

"We must open our doors to strangers. It is the rule."

Even horses and camels can get used to one another in time. Little by little the distance closed between Horse and Mustapha. And Moosa was able to tell her about the British teacher who had taught him good English and geometry and the poems of Robert Burns until her death the year before. He missed her still, he said. Comity realized that she must have been the white widow who had married a ghan... Except they were not ghans, were they? She must remember to tell her father that Moosa came from India, not Afghanistan. She must remember to tell her father how he had saved her from a wild camel and from eating frogs and getting lost in the desert and burned skinless, and had fetched her home and taken care of her and given her sweets and grapes and four yards of muslin. He had *tried* to save Fred, too.

Moosa told her of his plan (when he was rich) to make a stained glass window for the mosque at Calgo Crossing. He had seen one in a house door in Oodnadatta, and his teacher Mrs. Ameer had said that they were used in churches to make them beautiful. "It is important," he said, "to give some beauty back to Allah in return for all the beauty in the world."

And Comity resolved to be friends with Moosa, because he too understood about beauty, just as Fred had done. He even managed to be beautiful himself, like a fairy-tale prince who smelled of attar of roses and curry and had hands as large and delicate as fig leaves.

She also resolved to invite Moosa in when they reached Telegraph House, and give him orange juice and eggy fried toast, and rice pudding, and show him her mother's embroidery, and have him sit in the rocking chair on the verandah where he could unpack all his wonderful plans, like Hogg laying out his luggage.

Hogg!

How could she have forgotten? Quartz Hogg would be waiting at Kinkindele, with his big army pistol and his clutter of other weapons, smirking and smug, pleased with himself for shooting Fred, ruling the roost, strangling the chickens, holding the power of life and death over her and her father and all things to come.

"I cannot go home! I must tell the police: Mr. Hogg shot Fred! Take me to Oodna, not Kinkindele! I have to tell them! They have to arrest him! He's a devil! I cannot go back!"

Moosa Rasul considered this. The easy pace of his camel, the gentle flexing of his body forward and back in the saddle gave the impression of calm. Perhaps his kindness did not reach as far as Oodnadatta.

"This Hogg: he is a British devil?"

"Irish. Yes. But evil." And she tried to explain about the monster in the stationery store (even though that had been a mistake) and the not-working, and the piano playing and the pitch-and-toss, and bouncing her on his knees and being disrespectful to his superior, and holding a party and going on a hunt for Fred... And all the while she was talking, she felt the truth fall through the lattice of words and leave nothing Moosa would understand.

"The police will do nothing," said Moosa again. "Not for a jacky."

"You had better not come near the house," said Comity.

She *meant* to explain that Hogg shot people for talking

to her – foreign people – outsider people. But the terror was sitting so high in her throat that she only said, "Better not come near the house."

Kinkindele Repeater Station was a cluster of acacias and tea trees, spattered with blood-red desert peas. But for the slow turning of the windmill sails, it could have been a painting, though the goats were bleating.

"Thank you for the toothbrush."

"You are most welcome," said Moosa. He looked understandably hurt by her lack of hospitality.

"And everything," she added.

"You are most welcome."

She *meant* to explain that Quartz Hogg would probably kill her for throwing rocks at him. Or because she had seen him shoot Fred.

She *meant* to say that she did not want to marry Quartz Hogg – not in four years or five years or ninety-nine years! That Quartz Hogg had made himself king of Kinkindele. Then Moosa might have helped her, might have drawn the curved dagger he wore in his belt, and kept her safe from Quartz O'Malley Hogg.

But she knew what would happen. Hogg would shoot Moosa too, and tell people he knew the boy from back in Kabul and that Moosa had fought against the English and chopped up babies.

So she allowed Moosa Rasul to think she was a thankless, inhospitable child, to remount his camel and set out again on the long journey back to Calgo Crossing unrewarded. She failed to tell him that he looked like a fairy-tale prince and had almost saved her heart from crumbling to dust.

Comity dismounted, sore as a pulled wishbone. Horse was eager to get to the water troughs. He went ahead of her, through the gate of the yard, past the fallen wash-post, the grave-marker of Mary Pinny...

And the six newly dug graves alongside it.

CHAPTER SIXTEEN

Numbers

A massacre. Everyone she knew was dead. Everyone in her world had been murdered. What else could it mean? She turned to call out to Moosa, to fetch him back, but he was already out of earshot.

One, two, three, four…

She stood at the foot of the graves, all too sure of what had happened, but trying to guess at other explanations. An attack by native stockmen armed with porcelain-headed spears?

An electric storm? No buildings lay in ashes.

Leprosy? Not in two days.

A monster lurching from building to building, tearing

off the roofs and eating people as they fled? No roofs were missing.

…three, four, five, six, seven…

No. It was obvious. Quartz Hogg must have finished the work he started with Fred. He must have gone home and sat down by the forge and one by one picked off the wiremen, the blacksmith, the land manager and her beloved fa—

Hogg was probably sitting indoors now, doing tuneless, sucky whistling, waiting for "his little fiancée" to get home. Seven graves: Amos, Hart, Cage, Smith, Sankey, Mama and…

Who had dug these graves? They were so neat, so precisely spaced. But then Quartz Hogg was a finicky man – murderous, lazy and foul, yes, but finicky and precise. He must be the one who had marked them all with pebbles – that same way her mother used to prick fruit pies: C for cherry, A for apple…

A …H …C …S …S …

Already, illiterate snakes or lizards or chickens had scattered two of the markers, oblivious to the preciousness of names carried for a lifetime, identifying the uniqueness of each human soul.

Comity made a tour of inspection. The door of the stationery store stood open. There was nothing inside but a clutter of pots and pans, the fly screen off her bedroom window and two giant bedsprings.

The forge in the barn was not quite cold. She climbed to the lofts, found the wiremen's possessions; no sign of them, only their few belongings and the smell of their boots. Down below, Horse was snickering her adventures to her fellow wire-horses, but there was no one for Comity to tell…unless it was Quartz Hogg, king of Kinkindele, waiting at the table for his dinner.

What if he was out and about? She might just be able to creep in as far as the machine room and get off a message in Morse – STATION FOUR SOS SEND HELP – before Hogg returned and grabbed her or shot her dead.

Creeping along the verandah on hands and knees, her injured thigh screaming with pain, she peered in at the window. No one sat waiting at the table or dozing in the armchair. The piano was silent, the room almost tidy but for three cans of beans saluting her with raised lids.

She realized that she had crawled through a pool of whitewash spilled from a paint can, and remembered, in a rush, the luminous white cross dodging through the paddock as Fred ran for his life. The paint did not show on her white muslin, but it did leave a palm-print on the door handle as she opened the door.

184

A rattle of Morse, sharp as gunfire. Her body froze, but not her brain; it translated the signal.

...BORE PIPES FOR TEN WHIRLS PLUS...

It was almost as if, somewhere in the world, life was going on as normal.

The machine-room door was ajar. She could see a coil of cable, the heel of a shoe, heard the tap of the Morse key resending the message:

...PIPES FOR TEN WHIRLS...

He did not stop sending, even after she pushed open the door, because Regulations stated that a *message must be sent whole, at a regular speed, and without pauses.*

"Papa?"

"Home so soon, Comity? What is this you are wearing? I surmise that you went to the ghantown after all."

"Everybody is…" Comity gestured feebly towards the yard. "Everybody. Did the fellahs…?"

"The stockmen would appear to have gone walkabout. It would be a kindness to the cows and goats if you would milk them, please. Remind me to thank Fred for escorting you."

She continued to point back the way she had come. "Fred is dead," she said.

Herbert Pinny frowned and blinked several times. "Him too?" He seemed surprised, and rather disappointed in Fred. On the notepad by his hand, he had written the number 40 a dozen times over. He always fretted about numbers in a telegram. His eyes were bruised black for lack of sleep; his hands (blistered from digging) were ineffectually bandaged round with knotted handkerchiefs, and some new nervous habit had plucked out a large patch of hair from his temple. But his shoulders seemed less hunched than before, his lips less chewed. In fact, he seemed almost calm.

"Have you told anyone? Is anyone coming?" she asked.

Herbert turned back to his work. "Oh, I think we may manage on our own, may we not, Comity? We did before."

Amos, Hart, Cage, Sankey, Smith, Hogg… Comity could not blame her father for Hogg; hadn't she and Fred wished him dead? Hogg and Smith had both been bad servants of the British-Australian Telegraph Company. But Amos? And Hart? And Cage, with his seven distant sisters? Maybe Hogg had worked the others up to mutiny and violence, and Papa had had to fight for his life? Comity was desperate for some explanation that would make things be all right.

But Herbert Pinny was not available for comment. He had withdrawn not only to the machine room, but to somewhere deep underground, and Comity had no energy left to dig him out. You can try and try and try, but you won't get a burdi out of the ground – not once it has dug itself in. Fred had said that. A burdi has massive claws and clings on grimly to the dark and, in the end, the work is not worth it. You might as well leave the burdi alone in its burrow.

Besides, Comity *dared* not ask her father what had happened. He was all she had left in the world. What was she going to do? Send a telegraph to Head Office?

PAPA HAS KILLED EVERYBODY

Then state troopers would come and take him away, and he would go quiet and say nothing, like now, and forget to tell them how Aboriginal tribesmen had attacked with spears and done everybody to death. Or Afghans, like after the siege of Kabul. Or spiteful Tuckonies. Or the Devil-Devil.

So Comity fell in with her father's wishes, and kept house and milked the cows and the goats, and oiled the trap harness, and loosed the horses into the paddock and fetched them in again at night, and fed the chickens, and washed clothes and cooked and read…yes, even read, because *Ivanhoe* and *Little Women* filled up all those dangerous spaces in her head where thoughts might stow away.

And sure enough, a kind of peace settled.

At night, a tiredness took hold of her – a crocodile tiredness that seized her in its jaws and spun her downwards into a deep dark nothingness from which it was really difficult to swim up next morning. That was all to the good: sleep was a kindness.

Every night she locked the doors. Then she took to locking them after every trip into the yard for vegetables or washing or to feed the chooks. It seemed wise to lock up. In case the Aboriginals came back. Or the ghans.

Or the Devil-Devil.

Of course there had been no Kadimakara in the stationery store: Fred had seen inside and said so, and ever since then Comity had seen what a ridiculous idea they had cooked up between them. A man-made Kadimakara indeed! Silly nonsense!

But the Devil-Devil, who roams the world hunting down people who have done bad things, and tearing them limb from limb? Best to lock the door against the Devil-Devil. There were seven graves in the yard, and only one could be blamed on a tiger snake.

Now Herbert Pinny even allowed Comity to share the work in the machine room.

"Not numerals, of course. Never numerals," he said with a flicker of the old panic, because when people are telegraphing sums of money or head of sheep or times of trains, it is vital the numbers are transmitted accurately. Comity knew the rules as well as the Ten Commandments.

After dinner each night, she read to her father from *The Diary of a Nobody*. He appeared to listen, but it was hard to tell.

She thought about Fred every single day. Each night she looked at the moon and wondered if his soul really had made the leap up there – from the roof of the tin mosque, perhaps? As the days passed, and the full moon was pared down thinner and thinner, she felt a blind panic, in case Fred was left clinging to the last remnant of moon before dropping down screaming...

The screaming that came from the machine room was so terrible that Comity was sure her father had electrocuted himself.

Or the Devil-Devil had come.

She ran to her father's aid.

He was sobbing – head down and sobbing – a curled sheet from the notepad clutched in one hand, old notes from the metal spike strewn across the desk. His pencil jottings were gouged into the notepad, each number written and overwritten twenty times.

"*Papa! What's the matter? Tell me! What?*"

Herbert Pinny had been reprimanded by the Company for transmitting an incorrect numeral: 454 instead of 545. For the first time in his career, he had made an error. Just a slip, just a tiny mistake.

"Was it you, Comity? Was it your fault? Did you do it?" He grasped her wrists, terrifyingly hard, lips drawn back off his teeth, eyes searching her face for signs of guilt.

"But I do not do numbers," she said, feeling the small bones of her wrist crackle in his grasp. "I am not allowed."

The grip relented, and the face repented, and anger was replaced with abject horror. The fault was all his own. It was as if the whole world had collapsed – sky upon spire upon chimney upon roof upon man.

She persuaded him into his bed and left him there, wide-eyed, groaning with horror and whispering, "Five four five, five four five four five…"

The Morse machine stirred into life, like some Kadimakara built of metal and cabling. Comity fastened up her hair and went to take dictation from its rattling jaws.

CHAPTER SEVENTEEN

Happy Families

It was numbers or nothing after Herbert Pinny took to his bed. The laundry had to go hang. The chicken shed did not get cleaned out. When Starbuck cast shoes, Comity told him he would have to go barefoot. A possum got into the water butt and died there and she had to clear the blockage. Copying down numbers is easy in comparison with things like that.

And it was fine. It was all perfectly, absolutely, completely all right. Another Comity Pinny was living at Kinkindele and she was having a lovely time.

Dear Cousins,

Mama is very busy with the Sports Day. What a jolly time we are having! There are running races and high jump and long jump and handstanding and tite-rope walking and lassooing. (Cows are easier than horses becuase horses reer up.) There is a beayutiful golden cup for the winner. Frederick will win it naturelly. But he says I may have it if I want becuase he has gold crockery at home and things taist odd when you eat off it. Count Frederick is a very lively fella and can perform backward summersalts but not in his best uniform.

Unable to leave Telegraph House and roam the countryside, Comity loosed her imagination instead. Like an eagle, it soared over the places she had once gone with Fred, and reported back to her on the world's wonders.

Count Frederick did battle last week with a perentie lizard and felled it with a sling and five stones.

Mama says I must tell you: you have to be careful of wild camels. I got kicked in the thy and the scar is horrible even after weeks. Moosa said I was very brave.

Life is very quite here. The stockmen have gone walkabout. They do that. I do not know why.

When the camel train called at Kinkindele Repeater Station, Comity did not meet the eyes of the cameleers. She did not offer them refreshment, for fear they catch sight of the untidy kitchen, the unlit forge, the filthy chickens. If she could, she would have thrown a cloth over the seven graves, to hide them. Like a piano. If Moosa Rasul was among the cameleers, she did not see him, because she did not look.

She could manage to carry the bread, flour and the rice indoors. The crates of insulators and battery cells had to stay where they were in the yard: they were too heavy for her to shift on her own.

But back inside the house, everything was fine – absolutely and completely and totally and marvellously all right.

Dear Cousins,
Today I went to the Sea with Frederick. It is our favourite place, high up at the top of a hill. There are shells all over and perfect fish so you can count every singel bone.

Her pencil hung in the air. A drop of saltwater fell from her lashes onto the word *shell*, so that a scallop tasted saltwater again after aeons lying in the sun. It was such a long time since she had been to the Sea with Fred, and pored over the fossils and litter left high and dry by an ancient evaporated ocean. So strange: even Fred did not know a story big enough to explain it. Comity had described a real, wet ocean to him – what she remembered of one, anyway. And he had stared at her, marvelling at the immensity of her lies. In the end, two master storytellers had fallen silent, sitting, eyes shut, on the bed of an ocean, under shifting fathoms of imagined water, while whales swam by and the keel of Noah's ark left its white wake overhead.

If rememberings had not taken over from letter writing, Comity might have gone on to explain to the Blighs that she was talking fossils, archaeology... As it was, the Sea proved her undoing. For at last the noxious Blighs cried "Enough!" Sports days and fountains, dams and Russian counts, tightrope walkers and monstrous lizards had made them suspicious (sometimes a little envious) but one mention of the Sea, and Alexander, Anne and Albert all agreed: Comity Pinny was a liar.

Alexander wanted to sneak into his father's machine room and send the single word LIAR rattling from repeater station to repeater station to slap their cousin's silly face.

But Anne said no.

Cousin Anne had a better idea…

Life continued splendid – oh, better than splendid! – at Kinkindele. Really it did! There Comity sat in the machine room, her hair fastened up in a bun by two knitting needles, for all the world like her grandmother at the heart of her web of wool, strands of words stretching out on all sides, as she knitted together far distant lives. Good things were happening *everywhere*: weddings and business deals, babies and journeys and changes of address… Bad things were also happening everywhere – to everyone! – prison sentences, death and debt and temper and worry… And Comity was the one holding the reins. She was in control. It was almost as if she could allow or forbid the joys and tragedies to happen, because her hand was on the key.

All right, yes, the Devil-Devil was prowling the boundary fence, sitting on Goat Ridge in the moonlight and gluing emu feathers into vengeance shoes using gallons of blood. But Comity had a plan to deal with that too.

She was saving up tragedies on the metal spike by the Morse machine – all those messages about jilted sweethearts, children dead from measles, unpaid debts, sons in prison… She kept the spike by her bed. If, one night, the Devil-Devil leaped the fence and climbed through the window without a fly screen to tear her father to pieces, she would jump up and drive the spike into its chest. Not to kill it, of course – the Devil-Devil cannot be killed – but to *confuse* it with sadnesses. Sadnesses clog up the brain. Verily they do.

"Camels in the yard, Comity," she told herself, as the stately swaying ships-of-the-desert came into view. They emerged from their own dust cloud, scarred and overladen. Camels frightened her these days.

Going outside, she accidentally looked at the faces and recognized Moosa among the ghans, even though their heads were wrapped against a rising wind. They had all noticed their previous cargo still standing where it had been offloaded a month before. She felt ashamed – found out in her bad housekeeping.

"The wiremen are out on tour," she said. "Our fellahs have gone walkabout."

"I can help you, perhaps?" said Moosa, though the older men scowled at him.

"No! No. No, thank you. Father will see to it." And she took the mail and signed for the battery acid, flour, salt, paint, nails, copper wire and solder. When she reached for the mail, Moosa kept hold of it for a second or two.

"The gift of sweets prevailed." He leaned his head close to whisper it, and flashed her a smile as if she was expected to be glad too. "Allah is good."

"I expect so," said Comity.

"Is the hog-man still here?"

"No. No, he is gone. I cannot talk: I am very busy." And she snatched the letters and fled back into the house. For a long time the carriers stood about, discussing her – she could see them through the window, casting looks towards the house, faceless and frightening.

Among the deliveries were her twelve new message spikes. She had ordered them herself, using an official requisition form and forging her father's signature. That was good. Now she could booby-trap the verandah and maybe keep the monsters and ghosts from getting into the house.

There was also a letter from the noxious Blighs, addressed to Comity herself.

Charming cousin Comity,
Your letters have filled us with longing to see the wonders of Kinkingdeely. We have won round our parents with much pleading, and they have agreed to a trip. So we are setting off soon and hope to

arrive before Aunt Mary's birthday day.
Yours in exitement...

They had all signed it, artistic Albert adding a face beside his name. The face wore a big, smug smirk.

It was unthinkable, of course. They must not come. They had to be stopped. What could Comity say to put them off? That her father was ill? No! Then Superintendent Bligh would ask all sorts of questions. That typhus fever had carried off everyone? No! Superintendent Bligh would send a doctor. That the Devil-Devil had laid siege to Telegraph House? That there were seven graves in the yard? No. Whatever she did say must not fetch *anyone* to Kinkindele. And whatever the excuse, she would have to send it by telegram. There was no time for a letter to make the return journey: the Blighs were probably packing their bags at this very minute.

It had to be a vague and simple lie, but big enough to hide Kinkindele's secrets, like a cloth thrown over a piano. She worked out the Morse on the notepad and, when it was sent, burned the evidence.

DO NOT COME STOP

REGRET NATIVES AND CALGO GANS AT WAR

CHAPTER EIGHTEEN

The Big Lie

If only nice Mr. Boyce had been at his desk at Station Three. He would not have panicked. But for the first time in years, nice Mr. Boyce had gone on a sudden trip. His deputy telegrapher sent the message on to Station Two, with a slightly shaking hand. A war up near Station Four?

The news sped south across the empty Outback, onwards into Port Augusta, Adelaide and the Central Telegraph Office. It was delivered to the Bligh household, of course, but by then many other eyes had seen it, and the contents were so shocking that they quickly reached the Company President himself.

DO NOT COME STOP

REGRET NATIVES AND CALGO GANS AT WAR

South Australian Railways were told. The Government was informed. A war, however remote, must be snuffed out quickly, before it spread. Government property could be damaged! Innocent white Australians could suffer! The Wire could be severed! Order must be restored.

The Army was turned out.

Naturally telegrams were sent up the Wire asking for more details – for more information about this war. But a fault had developed somewhere between Stations Three and Five. All that came back was an anxious telegram from Mr. Boyce's wife at Three, saying that her husband was riding north to visit friends, and asking if he was "heading into danger". The failure of the Wire seemed like proof something was wrong.

General Gostard knew what he had to do. He and three hundred troopers of the South Australian Army boarded a train north out of Adelaide, heading for Oodnadatta. From there he would march north-west to Calgo.

Such things cannot be done secretly. Soon the parlours of Adelaide were buzzing with outrage.

"These ghans."   "Those blackfellahs."

"I was at Kabul and I can tell you…"

"They simply do not think like us."

"Not civilized."   "UnChristian."

"And warlike. Very bloodthirsty."

"If they only wore more clothes!"

"I tell you, when I was stationed in Kabul during the Afghan Wars…"

"We fetch these people here…"

"Well, not the jackies. We did not fetch them."

"Well no, not the jackies, obviously, but…"

"Need to be taught a lesson, and sharply too."

"If they *dressed* like us, they might *think* more like us."

During the Dreamtime, spiteful Marmoo invented insects and stuffed them into every crevice in the world. He must have invented rumours too: rumours breed just as fast as insects; they can infest an entire continent in no time.

Comity could never have guessed ten small words would multiply into three hundred troopers, three thousand bullets and a train trundling northwards.

Aunt Berenice sniffed her smelling salts and asked her children to be very brave: "Your aunt and uncle and little cousin Comity may be in serious danger. …But I cannot imagine why my sister thought we were planning to *visit* her. What sane person would travel needlessly to that dreadful, flyblown nowhere?"

Anne Bligh scowled at her brothers, warning them not

to say a word, then bent her head over her embroidery. She understood very well the reference to travel in the telegram, but nothing was going to make her confess. With any luck, Comity would get murdered by natives now, and no one need ever know about the letter Anne had sent her as a joke. Serve her right, the little liar.

CHAPTER NINETEEN

A New Eye

If only nice Mr. Boyce had been at his desk at Station Three when Comity sent the fatal telegram, all might have been well. But nice Mr. Boyce had startled everyone by going on a sudden trip. And why?

For months he had been growing increasingly troubled by the transmissions from Station Four. There were errors – nothing important: the numbers for instance were never wrong, not after that one official reprimand. But single letters were missed out, spelling errors regularly slipped in: BEAYUTIFUL and BECUASE, for instance.

Nice Mr. Boyce had three ears: two for train whistles, birdsong, his wife, etcetera, and one for Morse. This third ear was so finely tuned that he heard Morse like a human voice. Though they had not met for years, he knew Herbert Pinny's "voice" like that of a next-door neighbour. He knew when Herbert's assistant Leonard arrived – slow, methodical, a beginner. He knew when the assistant stopped transmitting and a lighter hand took over – a female hand perhaps? Sometimes the key was too lightly struck to register. Herbert's wife Mary, he assumed. Naturally Mr. Boyce had corrected any mistakes.

Boyce knew when a second assistant arrived a good while later: someone with a sending style as crisp as fresh lettuce. But over the weeks, this new hand sent fewer and fewer of the daily messages. The newcomer was clearly not pulling his weight.

Nice Mr. Boyce wished he could have corrected Herbert's 454/545 mistake, but of course there was no way of spotting it. Knowing Herbert from college days, he realized just what a blow the reprimand must have been to his friend.

It was shortly after this that Jack Boyce sensed a strange, light hand on the key at Station Four. Not Mary. No, not piano-playing Mary, who had transmitted Morse in delicate cadences, like music. (He had been worrying about Mary ever since she'd failed to thank him for the plants he'd sent her.) Could Herbert really be allowing his daughter to assist him? That was a disaster in the making!

"I think I may ride up to Number Four and check on Pinny," he told his wife, only half meaning it. He was not much of a travelling man.

"Ride all that way? At *your* age?" said his wife – which decided him then and there to go.

Mr. Boyce put in for leave, changed out of his dapper waistcoat and flannels and set off on the two-hundred-mile trip to Kinkindele with a horse, a pack horse and a tent. He followed the Wire, in the company of his own wiremen. When they reached the end of their section and turned back, he continued on his own, bivouacking beside a campfire every night with a horse breathing down his ear. He found it uplifting, eating supper under a canopy of stars and wearing baggy trousers for a change. The impossible vastness of the country impressed itself afresh on him as, day after day, he met no one. Why, it could swallow up a man, just as a man could swallow a gnat without noticing!

From a distance, Station Four looked very like Station Three transported into a different landscape. Twigs and leaves swish-rattled towards him in the rising wind and gave the impression of movement, but there was barely any. A pair of goats and four horses had turned their backs to the wind. A tablecloth caught in the branches of a tree flapped like a flag of surrender. The windmill that drove the generator was spinning at full tilt. Crates stood about in the yard, unopened. Five mangy chickens had pecked each other bald. Their droppings were alive with maggots.

And there were seven worrying mounds of dug earth, arranged in an orderly row.

"Holy angels," said Mr. Boyce to himself. "What happened here?"

Mary Pinny's pretty window boxes had been dragged into a double row in front of the mounds, and planks ripped out of the verandah had been stood on end, pinned upright by the window boxes. There were crudely daubed paintings on the planks: animals and stick people and birds. Nice Mr. Boyce drew the pistol he had brought along for rabbiting.

He negotiated the verandah, taking care not to step on any of the metal spikes or into gaps where the planks were missing.

"Herbert? Herbert Pinny?" he called, pushing open the door.

A girl holding a spanner came out of the machine room – a girl so sunburned, so unwashed and unbrushed, that he could not tell at first if she was European or Aboriginal, so thin and starved of sleep that her eyes were dark hollows. Greasy hair was screwed into a knot on top of her head and stuck through with two knitting needles. Her licked lips were like crumpled tissue paper, gummed at the corner with sores. Mr. Boyce put the pistol behind his back.

"Hello. I am Jack. I was at your parents' wedding. You must be Comity."

Meanwhile, the Army train set out for Oodnadatta, so crowded with troops that the brisk breeze blowing in at the window was a mercy. Beyond the Flinders Mountains, though, the windows had to be closed to keep out the gusting dust. The train driver and stoker wrapped their heads in cloths to keep the grit out of their ears.

"I am sorry. Papa is not available," said the little girl. "You could come back another day."

"Never mind," said Mr. Boyce. He nodded at the spanner in her hand. "Is this something you need help with?"

"The battery is dead."

"Oh dear. And the spares?"

"Dead too."

"Batteries are a trial, are they not? I am forever rebuilding mine. So…that means…the Wire is down, then?" (It was a blow to discover he could not dash off a message to Head Office or even share with his wife what he was seeing.) He tried to keep his voice light and calm, but the child's eyes swerved with panic.

"It will be mended soon. Papa will mend it."

"Well, I did see those big crates in the yard. I think they may be of use." And he tugged out the walking cane that was holding two cupboard doors shut, and went outside to break open the crate of battery cells.

Together, they began rebuilding one of the batteries. That is to say, Boyce rebuilt it while the child stood to one side, tapping with skinny little fingers on the desktop and trembling like a whippet. He did not try to take the spanner from her: he had a feeling it was as much weapon as tool. While he worked, he talked – as people do on the most normal of days. The girl's eyes drifted continuously to the window, the machine, the stopped clock.

"Those painted boards in the yard…" began Mr. Boyce.

"They keep the ghosts away from the house."

"The ghosts? Ah yes. I suppose they must… These batteries are something your wiremen could help you with. They out on patrol?"

"They're dead."

"Oh dear. What about your blacksmith?"

"Dead."

Boyce waited to regain full control of his voice. "And Herbert? Your pa? We went to college together, you know. He was quite the finest Morse man of our year." The girl did not answer. "And that lovely mother of yours?"

"There was a tiger snake in the wash basket," said the girl, winding a strand of greasy hair round her finger over and over and over again.

Mr. Boyce felt a sudden need to blow his nose, and turned aside. "What happened here, Comity?"

But the child only shrugged.

The bad-tempered wind blustered round the house, bringing down wisps of thatch. As each reed floated past the window, Comity Pinny would flinch and tighten her grip on the spanner.

"Who are you expecting, Comity? Aboriginals? Blackfellahs, I mean? With spears?"

"Oh no!" said Comity. "The Kinkindele mob went walkabout."

"Because...?"

She shrugged again. "Because they do."

Boyce was running out of calm. "You must have seen *something*, my dear?"

"I was in tintown with Fred." She straightened the

torn-off pages on their metal spike until they lined up neatly.

"What, you were kidnapped by the ghans?"

"No! Of course not! I went there with Fred."

"Ah. And where is this Fred now?" enquired the telegrapher gently.

"Dead. Mr. Hogg called him a dingo and shot him."

Boyce almost laughed with relief. "Fred was your pet dog!"

She scowled ferociously at him. "No. Fred was my best friend."

Generally there are two acid batteries in use and one in the repair shop. Boyce deduced that for all three to be dead, some time must have passed since routines went to pot at Station Four.

"Your pa's deputy not up to snuff, then? Did he walk out?"

"No. He's dead."

"Ah."

"I do not know which grave is him. There was an aitch, but it might have been H for Hart or H for Hogg."

"Indeed it might."

"Or I would burn him in the ground with kerosene."

To hide his tears and terror from the child, and to stop himself tormenting her with more questions, Jack Boyce went to look around the house. And just when he had begun to think everyone but Comity was dead, he came across someone else who was not.

"*Pinny?* Pinny, are you all right? What happened here? Are you wounded? Poor, dear Mary! I am so sorry, man, so very sorry!"

Slumped on his bed, Herbert Pinny did not so much as open his eyes. Perhaps, after all, he too was dead.

Even when Herbert did stir, his lips were slack and his eyes sunken and unfocussed. There were glasses and cups all over the room. Boyce snatched the blanket off the man and bundled it out of the window, nervous of fleas or lice. It was a blessed relief to find his friend alive, but Boyce's compassion was hampered by anger. "Are you *drunk*, man? Are you so drunk that your daughter must run the whole station? For pity's sake, are there any Regulations in the book that you have *not* broken?" He tried to raise Herbert to his feet, but the man was limp as treacle.

"Papa does not drink," said the child, who had followed him and stood now in the bedroom doorway. "He is a telegrapher. And an abstainer. He does not drink."

Boyce snorted, no longer able to master his disgust. His gesture took in the litter of glasses and cups. "What are these, then?"

Comity scratched at her hair with the spanner and

dislodged one of the knitting needles. "Pituri. You use it to catch emus. But I did not use so much, because Papa is smaller than an emu."

"For the love of God! Why would you do such a thing? Why would you drug your own father, you unnatural child?"

Comity frowned, startled by his sudden noise and puzzled that she needed to explain. "In case he wanted to kill me too, of course," she said.

CHAPTER TWENTY

What Happened Here

Slowly, painfully, Herbert Pinny emerged from his stupor like a hatching turtle surfacing from under sand. He thought he might die of it. His head felt as cracked and fragile as an egg.

"There was a party," he said, and Boyce threw a cup to the floor in disgust. Alcohol was behind this, after all. That drink should have corrupted a man like Herbert, once so clean-living!

And indeed, alcohol had been behind it, as Herbert went on to explain.

*

Behind the locked doors of the stationery store, deputy telegrapher Quartz Hogg had secretly built a still – a distillery – for the illegal manufacture of liquor. He intended to sell it to the local Aboriginals and generally use it to liven up "this dust bowl of boredom", as he put it. He organized some of the stockmen to bring him the ingredients, promising hooch whisky in exchange. When there were supplies enough of whisky, Quartz Hogg announced his intention to have a party.

"I got Comity away, fearing this party would be an uncouth affair. I knew nothing of the alcohol brewing in the yard, but there was something devilish in that man – something dangerous. I wanted Comity away from here."

Barricaded in the back room, Herbert Pinny had soon heard the clink of glasses, and smelled alcohol. He had shouted his objections through the door – forbidden his staff to drink, citing Company Regulations. He was ignored. Quite quickly, men who were meant to take their every command from the Stationmaster were roaring drunk and beyond hearing anything he said. Somehow – Pinny did not know how – Hogg had offended the Aboriginal guests, who left. (Not being witness to it, Pinny could not say quite what had happened, but there had been shouting out in the yard.) The permanent residents of Repeater Station Four were left to revel on their own: Hogg, Smith, Amos, Hart, Cage, Sankey…

The party had lasted all night.

At some point, Hogg and Smith had disappeared and were gone for a couple of hours. Coming back to find the punchbowl empty, Smith went to the stationery store to replenish it. It was pitch-dark in the one-time chapel, but Smith added liberal flavouring to the hooch from the various ingredients lined up on the shelves: fruit juices, berry compote, home-made cider brewed in a bucket… Drunk and fumbling, unfamiliar with Hogg's still, and in inky darkness, it was an easy mistake to make. Battery acid in place of cider? Kerosene or sheep drench in place of fruit compote? Who could say?

No one who swallowed the whisky-punch that night would ever say anything again.

The only person not to drink the poisonous concoction, of course, was teetotal Herbert Pinny, imprisoned in his office. So the next morning he was not, like the others, lying dead in the living room, the barn or the yard.

"Hogg was the last to die. I heard him cursing and crying out for many hours. He demanded I help him, but I could not open the door of the machine room, of course, and neither could he, not once the pains were upon him.

He wanted to reach the machine, and telegraph for help. But he had gone to such pains to ensure the door was very thoroughly barred."

"You might have telegraphed yourself?" whispered Jack Boyce, but Herbert must not have heard the question.

"I could hear Hogg moving about the house, looking for relief, looking for Comity, calling on Comity. He seemed to think that something was chewing on him – some animal – devouring him, and that she could maybe loosen its jaws… I am glad I got her away. It was not a thing for a child to hear…"

Forcing the office window out of its frame, Herbert Pinny finally clambered out of the machine room and began to make sense of what had happened to the staff of his station.

"Hogg was in the dunny – half in, half out of the dunny. He seemed delirious – begging me to 'get the dogs off' him – 'drag the dogs off' him. The moon was full and I believe he mistook it for a face. Kept pointing up at it, saying that there he was: *the man who set his dogs on me to chew up my guts*. I tried to go to his aid – of course I did! To move him out of the dunny, at least: no one should die in a dunny. But of a sudden, he took it into his head that it was I who had poisoned him. *You wanted rid of me, Pinny, but I'll outlive you yet!*' And he took me by the throat, and his strength did indeed seem restored for I quite believed, in that moment, that he and not I would live to see daylight.

"The snake must have been drinking from the bucket. There is always water kept in a bucket by the toilet – I am sure you do the same. Our struggles overturned the bucket and the snake (I suppose) struck out in fear… Hogg was bitten in the throat… Soon after that, he was spared his suffering. Dead. It was a tiger snake, I believe."

Herbert Pinny had then set about burying the bodies. The labour had half killed him, especially with the glaring immensity of land and sky watching him as he dug. Watching him, watching him, watching him, watching him, watching him dig.

"And you thought to tell no one all this? To signal no one?" said nice Mr. Boyce.

Herbert looked at him in disbelief. He cupped his hand, as if round a Morse key. "How could I hold the words in my hands, Jack?" he said. "How could anyone?"

The machine rattled an acknowledgement from Station Three:

WELCOME BACK ON LINE FOUR STOP
GOD BE PRAISED

There was more besides. An urgent message from the

Superintendent's Office in Adelaide regarding the war.

"WAR?" Jack Boyce read and reread the letters he had just taken down on the notepad. "There is a WAR?"

"Oh. No." Comity giggled, embarrassed. "There is not a war, really and truly."

"But the Army has been sent to quash it! They are coming north aboard a train now!"

The two men stared at Comity, but she was beyond regret, beyond apologizing. She had just found out that her father had *not* killed six people. He had not killed *anyone*, and the relief was so huge that she thought the wind around the house must be the sound of cheering. What was one little lie in a good cause?

"I had to say there was a war," she explained. "I had to stop the Blighs visiting. They are noxious, you see. And they would have spoiled everything."

Mr. Boyce looked around him in dismay and wondered if there was anything at Kinkindele left to spoil.

He telegraphed at once to correct the error.

DISREGARD UNTRUE RUMOUR OF WAR

But it was too late to stop the troopers, who were already aboard their train and heading north, uncontactable. But they would find out when they got to Oodna. There would be the happy fact of a telegram waiting: DISREGARD UNTRUE RUMOUR OF WAR

"Not if they take the Calgo Spur," said Herbert.

"Then we'll telegraph the place," said nice Mr. Boyce, moving towards the machine room.

"There's no wire to Calgo."

Comity said it was not a problem. "I can go to Calgo Crossing, and if the Army come there, I can tell them I made a mistake." She had begun to sense panic in the room, but could not quite join in with it. She was far too happy. After all, her father had escaped being poisoned! Quartz Hogg had caused his own death! The Devil-Devil was not going to come bursting through the wall in shoes of bloody feathers, and rend Herbert Pinny limb from limb! Her father did not need to kill her to cover up his guilty crimes, because he had not done any crimes. Besides, there was no war. She went to get her parents' wedding photograph, to see if nice Mr. Boyce was in it.

Herbert, speaking under his breath, took the chance to ask his friend, "What do you think the Army will do when they arrive?"

Mr. Boyce had been asking himself the same question. Unless the officer in command *did* receive a telegram recalling him, he would arrive like the wrath of God. Even a complete lack of brandished spears, flying bullets or bodies in the street would not be enough to deter an army ablaze with righteous indignation and spoiling for a fight.

The cattle ranchers in the Bush, the nervous folk in the cities would *expect* it. Wherever the rumours of war had reached, fear and bigotry was bound to be rife. This would be the perfect excuse to expel the unChristian cameleers, the perfect excuse to persecute the Aboriginals.

"What will they do?" said Mr. Boyce. "Hang a few Aboriginals. Burn down Calgo. That's my guess. Something. Anything rather than have a wasted journey and look stupid. They're on a punitive mission: they are bound to find something to punish."

In the doorway, Comity dropped the framed photograph she was holding, and its glass cracked. "But they cannot! What about Moosa?"

What about Moosa's little sisters and kind mother? What about the thoroughbred Australian camels and the mosque hung with embroidered cloths; the washing lines where long robes fluttered in the breeze like rows of angels.

"The fellahs have done nothing! There is no war!"

And yet Fred had done nothing, and Quartz Hogg had still shot him.

The boards propped up between graves and house fell over one by one. The wind, with snarling ferocity, was circling Telegraph House. Perhaps, like the Devil-Devil, it could smell guilt – Comity's guilt. She had told a lie, and the lie had grown: from the size of a telegram to the size of a war. The seven graves in the yard were nothing. Wait till the Army had finished with the menfolk of Calgo Crossing and the Kinkindele mob.

CHAPTER TWENTY-ONE

No Day to be Out-of-Doors

The same wind had overtaken the troop train. The windows had been shut tight, but the sand still came in through the coachwork, glittering gold in mid-air, but settling into a rime of grit on every seat, uniform, kitbag and crate of ammunition. The driver and stoker in the cab drew their headcloths over their eyes and were able to see only the glowing shape of the furnace door through the fabric. Now and then the iron-rimmed wheels slipped on rails covered in sand and sent a shudder down the length of the train. The soldiers cursed all ghans and blackfellahs for choosing to live in this ashtray of a land.

*

Nice Mr. Boyce sent a reassuring message down the Wire to his wife. At least he hoped it was reassuring. Morse messages have no tone of voice. It was something he had often found regrettable: that he could not lend the words an encouraging upbeat or a soothing softness.

Suddenly the door of the machine room pushed open and he was confronted by a woman demanding his clothes.

"Dirty man smell," said the woman. "Give shirt."

Loud Lulu had come for the washing. Entirely forgetting she had been dismissed by Smith, she had arrived, zealous as ever, at Telegraph House and had already pulled the tablecloth off the living room table, scattering empty bean cans. "This place stink bad," she said.

When Hogg had told the locals to gather him ingredients for liquor, a surprising number had turned him down, saying the ancestors frowned on alcohol. But they were content to keep quiet about the still. Only the laundress "Loud Lulu" had made trouble. Lulu had as ferocious a hatred of strong drink as the Stationmaster. Her son had taken to drinking, spent all his money on it and managed to ruin his life. Finding out about the whisky-still in the stationery store, Lulu had thrown one of her screaming fits, and Smith had fired her then and there, before she could give the game away and ruin the fun for everyone.

Hogg had also forbidden anyone to speak to Fred, for

fear he found out about the still and snitched to the Stationmaster's daughter. As a result, Fred had been frozen out by his own mob without knowing why. Fred's own father (a hard-drinking man) had been the first to shun him.

Chuntering and fuming, Loud Lulu had taken off on a walkabout through her ancestral landscape. There she had recovered her temper, forgotten all about being sacked, and returned to Kinkindele. Where she had been keeping herself till now was anybody's guess, but here she was, come for the laundry again.

"Shirt! Shirt! Give me shirt, dirty boy!"

Mr. Boyce offered her afternoon tea.

"Can you find your mob?" he asked her, once she was sitting down at the table, the laundry clutched in her lap.

"No."

Comity and her father joined them. For tea.

"I know they are on walkabout, but would you be able to find them – or get a message to them?" said Mr. Boyce.

"No." Lulu's voice was as loud as a door slamming.

"We need their help, you see," said Pinny.

"Many day far off," said Lulu implacably. "Many, many, many."

"They need not worry about the man who shot the child Fred. Hogg is not here any more."

Lulu's eyes flickered in the direction of the yard. "No. Dead in the ground, him," she said with some relish. (Not so ignorant of *some* facts, then.)

Comity filled Lulu's cup again. "But his ghost, Lulu. His ghost is making mischief. Big damn mischief," said Comity sweetly. "Could you maybe ask the ancestors to take a message? The ancestors must know where our fellahs are." Fred had told her how thoughts could be thrown, like a spear from a woomera, far into the dark places of the world. She would have done it herself had she known how.

The train slowed to a crawl. The sand flying past the window made it hard to tell if they were moving at all. Vibration and thuds might be the passage of the train over the rails or the wind pitching uprooted shrubs against the wheels. The sand on the floor of the carriage was ankle deep.

The troopers were of the opinion that the storm must have scotched the war before it had really got started. Surely neither side would even be able to find each other in the dust. The train might as well take them back to Adelaide.

Their sergeant told them they were not paid to have

opinions, and that they were a pack of lily-livered rabbits. The train would be pressing on, come what may.

Then the train driver sent word that he was stopping: there was an escarpment up ahead and wild camels were herding together on the track, sheltering from the wind.

There was a certain amount of cheerful laughter. It did not last.

Mr. Boyce harnessed the trap. Even in blinkers, Starbuck did not want to leave the barn. This was no day to be out-of-doors. A gust of wind struck the cart so hard that it shifted sideways on its wheels: it would have been better with the weight of two men aboard rather than one. But Jack Boyce knew he was on his own: Pinny was barely fit to stand, let alone make the journey to Calgo Crossing in this weather.

"Tell your pa to secure his windmill while I'm gone," Boyce suggested to Comity, who was trying and failing to trap the chickens in the stationery store. "This wind will spin it off its moorings if he's not careful."

Dismayingly, Comity said, "I shall do it. Papa does not go out of doors."

"What *never*?"

"He is curlew-cursed."

"Ah."

"Though I do not know why he should be. He never killed anybody's children."

"No! Absolutely not."

"Wait while I do the windmill," said Comity. "I am coming with you. I know some people in Calgo."

Nice Mr. Boyce tried to forbid it. He was not an adventurous man and his heart quailed at the thought of driving into a dust storm in the fragile hope of finding a ghantown before the Army did. But the idea of taking along a little girl was unthinkable!

"Fred and I went there. They do not like mixing the sand and the salt, but Moosa does not mind us. We have to say nice things about his dates and his toothbrushes and his camels. And wash your hands. They are very particular."

Boyce looked at the gypsy waif with the matted hair, fixed frown and the panic in her eyes. Momentarily, back there in the house, she had put on happiness, but then she'd been forced to take it off again, like Cinderella robbed of her trip to the ball.

"None of this is your fault, Comity," he said.

She was startled by his stupidity. "Of course it is. All of it."

Caught by the wind, the paint can by the door of the house rattled along the verandah. It put white drops of paint onto the toecaps of Herbert Pinny's shoes as he stepped outside. Reflexly, he tried to wipe each shoe down the back of the opposite trouser leg. Too dizzy to manage it, he leaned on the rocking chair – which tilted him further off-balance. He could have been mistaken for a drugged emu.

"Drive," said Comity, climbing aboard the trap. She did not want nice Mr. Boyce to see that terrible moment when her father turned from a stationmaster into a cowering, terrified child.

The train did not hit the gum tree. The gum tree hit the train, wedging itself under the front wheels. It must have travelled a great distance to do it, because the landscape (as far as anyone could see it) was empty of trees. The stoker said it was a miracle, because, when he got down to cut it loose, he could see that the rails up ahead had been swept away by flash flooding. A minute more and the train would have been derailed, perhaps even overturned. The driver sent word to the officers' car that he would be reversing, back towards Adelaide.

But General Gostard was not prepared to be defeated by trees or washouts or a flurry of dust. He ordered the driver to reverse only as far as the Calgo Spur.

"Calgo Spur? Cannot recommend that, sir. No one uses it. Impassable, like as not. It's not seen any maintenance for a year or more. Sorry state it's in."

"We shall take it as far as it will take us. If we meet with misfortune, we shall disembark and march cross-country!" the General announced, as though he had been fighting campaigns in this part of the world since he was old enough to pull on boots.

The troop train did indeed find the flimsy branch line and steam halfway along it but, finding its rails equally strewn with sand, came to a halt in a stony wilderness, rocking on its wheels in the wind. The driver tried to reverse, but the track was so smothered in dust that the wheels rolled quite smoothly off the rails and sank into the ground.

"Where the devil are we?" asked three hundred men, then answered themselves: "Middle of Nowhere."

Only with sundown did the wind relent. Mr. Boyce and Comity stopped at the mound springs when murk turned to darkness, and waited for moonrise in the hope they could press on. The journey from Kinkindele had taken far too long! The Army must surely have arrived in Oodna by now – must surely have received a telegram recalling them and got back on their train, peaceful as lambs. Anything else did not bear thinking of, so, as far as possible, neither of them did.

The wonderful Land of the Moon was grimy now, with grit covering every flower petal and bird nest – even the water. It was as if Bahloo had neglected his housekeeping and let the dust settle.

"Fred wanted his spirit to jump up from here and live on the moon," Comity said. "But it is only rock, isn't it, Mr. Boyce?"

Jack Boyce bedded down under the cart. His weary skeleton settled into the contours of the ground. He planned to think through Herbert Pinny's problems and come up with a solution or two. Instead, he was asleep in moments. Woken by the sound of crying, he rolled out from between the wheels to find Comity sobbing, terrified, pointing a shaking finger at the moon. "Does that mean the world is going to end?"

The moon had come up as red and glowing as a giant ruby.

He put a comforting arm round her. "Is that your friend Fred talking nonsense again?"

Comity was shocked. "No! It is in the Bible! When the moon comes up blood-red, the world is going to end!"

Nice Mr. Boyce bit his lip. "Or so much dust is

suspended in the air between us and the moon that it has coloured-in the gold." His own heart was swelling at the sheer beauty of the red-tinted night. "It is quite like stained glass, look. The rose window in a cathedral… Should we press on since the wind has dropped?"

Comity dared not admit just how unwilling she was to press on. For now she was thinking of Moosa's dream of stained glass in the tin mosque, and how she might have smashed it with one little lie.

From somewhere nearby came the belch of a camel in the darkness and Comity was convinced the wild one had come back. Mr. Boyce took the safety catch off his pistol. Best to be prepared.

The feeling that they were being followed persisted all the way to Calgo Crossing.

The wind had swept the gossips and goats and washing and children off the streets and into the houses. The place seemed deserted. It all looked so different under a dust-draped sky: Comity could not even identify Moosa's home. Cane straw drifted into their faces from the roof of the mosque. The silence seemed ominous, but there were no buildings burning, no bodies strewn about. Oh, the relief!

The Mullah came out at last – the one who had thought

it a bad idea to have Comity stay in Calgo. He was thinking it now, too.

"Allah ho Akbar," said the Mullah warily.

"He is risen indeed," said Jack Boyce. "We have come to avert a small calamity."

"*Moosa! Moosa Rasul!*" Comity, looking over her shoulder and spotting her redeemer through the gloom, jumped down from the trap and ran. Mustapha the camel sashayed nervously sideways. Nostrils closed against the dust, he looked more hoity-toity than ever. "Oh, Moosa! Thank goodness!" She hugged his leg, which was the only part of him she could reach. Everyone was startled: tempers bristled at the sight. Moosa Rasul was more surprised than anyone. For though he had followed the pair all the way from the mound springs, fearful for their safety, he had not expected to be thanked for it.

His delivery run to Kinkindele Station had troubled him. The mounds like graves, the missing stock, the crates still standing in the yard: they all spoke of trouble. But Comity's refusal to speak, to look at or even to hear him out had left him powerless to help. Comity had made it very plain he was neither wanted nor welcome.

"If the Army come here I will tell them it is all my fault!" said the girl clutching Moosa's leg. "I told a lie! I said there was a war! I am so sorry!"

232

*

The Army had not reached Calgo. They had not even reached the mainline railhead at Oodnadatta. Those waiting to meet them at Oodna worked out that the troop train must have taken the Calgo Spur – bad choice. By now the rails would have been rubbed out by the dust storm. Three hundred men were marooned somewhere in the desert. But where?

The matter was put beyond doubt when a messenger arrived from Oodna, on horseback, asking the help of the cameleers to *find and assist those in peril of their lives*. It was not so much a request as a Government demand.

So now the menfolk of Calgo Crossing must go and rescue an army sent to punish them for something they had not done! As they mustered and muttered on the main street, the glances they cast at Comity were full of resentment and hurt. Word of her "mistake" had rippled outwards through the town and the gossips had simplified it: the girl had told a lie about the ghans, and summoned the Army to kill them. Women in the doorways narrowed their eyes at her and told themselves how right the Mullah had been: it had been foolish to shelter outsiders, even outsiders in need.

Moosa Rasul, who had been more kind than anyone,

233

could not conceal his bewildered hurt. "Why?" he said. "Why did you say these things about us? You leave your friends behind as a camel leaves its dung."

No one had ever said anything so terrible to her. Tears burned grittier in her eyes than all the dust had done on the ride. It was far too difficult to explain about the telegram, and a poor enough excuse at that. But time was so short! Let them banish her into the Outback to be eaten by wild dogs – but not just yet! Not till she had to put a stop to the war!

"We have to show the Army that ghans and the fellahs are friends – when you find the Army, I mean. We have to show them ghans and fellahs all getting on as happy as galahs in a gum tree!"

Moosa gave a snort of disdain at her absurd wishful thinking. The Aboriginals and the tintowners liked each other about as much as horses liked camels.

"...except the Kinkindele mob's on walkabout! Loud Lulu has gone looking for them, but she may forget to look because some days her brains are in upside-down! You got a mob of blackfellahs living round these parts, Moosa Rasul? Any mob! On my bended knees, be kind!" Her voice was so shrill that Mustapha the camel tried to move away from it, circling and circling to shake off the annoying little creature clinging to its girth.

Moosa Rasul looked down at her from his great height. "You should ask your *friend* Fred," he said cuttingly, and rode off down Calgo's main street.

Comity stood desolate and distraught, as the street filled up with camels, and the search party of cameleers tacked up and made ready for their expedition. At the other end of the street, Moosa turned in his saddle.

"Well? Are you coming?" he called, and she trotted after him without knowing why, jumping over little mounds of manure in the roadway. *You leave your friends behind as a camel leaves its dung.* The words rattled around in her head.

Moosa dismounted by the cemetery, and it suddenly occurred to Comity that he was serious about her asking Fred's help. He was planning to *summon up Fred's spirit.*

Was that what Muslims did? Comity had no idea. Comity had kneeled beside her mother's grave in the yard, talking to Mary Pinny, telling her the news and so on. She had even asked Jesus to fetch Mama back to life. But summon up ghosts? That was witchy and expressly forbidden, and definitely against Regulations. Even so…

If Moosa knew a way for her to talk to Fred's ghost, she would dare damnation to do it, she missed him so much.

As row upon row of iron bedsteads came into view, Comity's heart thudded and squirmed in her chest. Would they have to dig up Fred's body in order to speak to his spirit? And even if Moosa knew some perfumed Punjabi magic to raise up ghosts, would Fred choose to come back from the afterlife? Seeing as Comity had let him down so badly.

They passed the last of the bedsteads without stopping at any of the graves, and reached the date orchard beyond. No, of course, thought Comity. Ghans would not bury an Aboriginal in Muslim ground.

"Fred. *Fred!*" called Moosa Rasul. "*Ngai ouri!*" It seemed a pitiful poor kind of ritual compared with putting on body paint and dancing and chanting in rhyme for two hours under a midday sun...and that had just been to summon up Tuckonies. The wind plucked at Moosa's robes like hands; it stood Comity's matted hair on end; it tugged at the date palms and shook loose a sprinkling of fruit. It shook a camel-skin shelter propped up on flimsy branches in the heart of the orchard. "*Ngai ouri, Fred!*"

A figure, as twiggy and bristle-topped as a Punjabi toothbrush, emerged from the shelter and blinkered both his eyes against the flying dust. It was not a ghost, because it was holding a book and who ever heard of ghosts reading?

"*Fred?*" said Comity.

"Lilly-pilly?" said Fred. "You in trouble? You look like dead burdi I dig up one time."

236

*

Fred. It burst against Comity's tongue like sugar every time she said it. His name was, and always would be, inextricably bound up with sugar. Apparently, when someone is sick in the Punjab, his family send gifts of sweets to all the children in the village:

"To balance the forces of joy and sadness," said Moosa. "Of course medicine too is important. But medicine and prayers work better when the forces are balanced. I thought you understood this."

Comity remembered her washed and mended clothes being handed back to her, neatly folded, a packet of sweets balanced on top, so prettily wrapped.

"No! I thought Fred was dead! I thought the sweets were supposed to make me feel better!"

Moosa nodded. "This explains your coldness when I brought you news. That the sweets had prevailed. I thought it strange."

"They *were* very good sweets," said Comity, "only I did not know how good!" And she laughed again, like a mad person. She could not stop herself. Last time in Calgo she had cried – cried while people spoke to her, cried while they ate, cried while people were praying... Now all she could do was laugh. There was a definite need for a better balance between joy and sadness: this up-and-down was exhausting.

She and Fred leaned against one another as they walked: Comity wanted proof that he was not a spirit, and he was supplying it. Also, both were rather like rotten fence posts which will only hold up if they lean heavily against each other.

Comity explained her Big Mistake yet again, for Fred's benefit.

"Ah! The noxious Blighs!" said Fred, full of sympathy.

Moosa, who was a stranger to lying, was less impressed. "Such a very BIG lie," he murmured.

"It grew big to cover up the little ones," said Comity. "Sometimes that happens."

Fred was adamant: "Awake-dreaming is *not* lying," he said. "You send noxious Blighs your most excellent stories. They damn lucky beggars. They should be glad. Jesus should to send bears."

"Bears?" said Moosa, hardly liking to ask.

"To eat them up. Like Mr. Elisha in the Bible. He call bears to eat up noxious children. Verily he did."

Moosa shook his head and laughed. As a dutiful son, he had resolved to dislike and mistrust all Aboriginals as much as his family and neighbours did. But Fred's wild stories and ridiculous beliefs had worn Moosa down bit by bit. No one in Calgo had wanted to house him once he was healed, but Moosa had installed him in the family orchard, citing the laws of hospitality until he got his way. *Why? He is only a jacky!* his aunts and uncles had said. But Fred could not simply be stowed in a crate labelled *Jacky*; he was a true original. And undeniably all-Australian.

"We have to stop the Army," Comity explained to Fred. "We have to find them wherever they are, and tell them there is no war and it's all my fault."

"The Army must be found; this much is true," said Moosa. "If their train is mired on the Calgo Spur, they need water and rescue. If they leave the train, they may lose themselves and die. We men of Calgo will fetch them safe home and tell them there is no war. If they doubt us, we will need the proof you suggest." Moosa winced when he said it.

"Yes! When the Army get here they shall see 'mullah' and 'jacky' sitting together on the ground, in perfect harmony."

"They will?" said Fred dubiously.

"They might," said Moosa grudgingly, "if you can find any jackies." He was practical and organized and very impressive for a boy of sixteen or seventeen. But whenever he spoke to Comity, any warmth had gone out of him, doused by Comity's Big Unnecessary Lie. "You, Miss Comity, and Mr. Boyce must stay here: pony and cart are no good for the journey. The ground is either deeply soft or there is gibber stone all over."

"Lend us horses, then, Mr. Rasul," said Comity. "I have to come."

CHAPTER TWENTY-TWO

Gostard's Last Stand

Fred's assignment was to find a mob – any mob of fellow "fellahs" – and take them back to Calgo to create a picture of perfect peace whenever the Army chose to put in an appearance. So far, he had found the bones of an eagle, a feral pig, a cat tree festooned with corpses, a nest of centipedes and nine green emu eggs. But he had not seen a soul. He asked the landscape, shaped as it was from the bodies of his ancestors, but his ancestors held their tongues, threw dusty wind in his face and shunned him. He shouted his request up at the sky – "A mob! Any mob!" – but perhaps his breath smelled too much of Calgo hospitality for Byamee to listen.

Suddenly and unaccountably, he began to be afraid: not for himself, but for Comity and Moosa. He abruptly stopped looking, and set off towards the Calgo Rail Spur. Not that he knew where it was.

He should have retraced his steps as far as Calgo and asked for directions, but there was no time.

Suddenly he was convinced of it: there was no time.

The silvery acacias were pointing their shining twigs towards the horizon; the leaf litter rattling round his feet told him to pick up his heels. The shadows lapping from under the rocks seemed to point the way he should go, and the birds tumbling on the wind shouted, *There! There!* He ignored the nagging pain in his chest and loped in the direction (he hoped) of a derelict railway track.

To his astonishment he found it. To his even greater astonishment, he saw ahead of him, also heading towards the line, the dust-smudged figures of an Aboriginal mob. The quiet murmur of singing came to him on the wind: singing and a familiar bad-tempered chunter of swear words.

"*Lulu?*" he called, and the laundress turned and looked at him.

Considering she thought she was seeing a ghost, she did not scream very loudly at all.

*

242

Aboard the train, water was rationed now. What had seemed like a temporary hold-up had become a marooning. Sand had blown in to such a depth that the train could not budge. A full regiment of men were available to dig it out, but with five shovels between them, numbers did not count for much.

Thirst, the cruel landscape and the smell of gun oil stirred up memories of the Afghan War – in the older men at least. They shared their reminiscences, which were mostly grim and bloody and did nothing to raise the spirits of men marooned in a train in a dust storm, on a defunct branch line, in the Middle of Nowhere.

The windows were so caked that there was no seeing out. The seats and floor were a uniform sand colour, and the field rations were grit sandwiches. Every gust of wind jarred the carriages and shook a caster sugar sprinkling of sand out of the luggage nets.

As soon as the wind dropped, the plan had been to disembark and set off on foot for Calgo.

"Should've done it last night," one soldier muttered. "Wind dropped, and there were stars." He was Outback-born and could steer by the stars when there was a need. General Gostard, however, was a city man and saw no use for the stars, especially with the nights so bitter cold and his officer's bunk so warm. Gostard had put off disembarking till morning…and with morning, the wind had returned.

The train guard came by outside, creaming sand off the windows with a broom. So the landscape revealed itself to the men inside in horizontal stripes: sky at first, then sparse tops of gum trees, camel heads, turbans, rifles…

"The ghans are on us!" shouted a voice cracked with thirst.

From his own point of view, the guard with the broom uncovered a row of faces stricken with alarm – men reaching for their packs – men reaching for their weapons. He turned to see what had caused their panic, and enjoyed the blessed sight of a ghan rescue party swaying towards the train. It was a Christmassy picture – two dozen magi on camels, bearing gifts and towing spare horses. To the guard, the cameleers were just about as welcome as Christmas Day.

Then the windows of the train started clattering down, and rifles were bayoneting the air.

"No!" cried the guard, waving his arms over his head. "They've come to—" He felt the heat of a bullet sear past his hand, and smelled cordite. A camel stumbled, screamed and unseated its rider.

Shoot at a rescue party?

Enraged ghans produced rifles of their own – ancient

ones manufactured in the Punjab and modern ones made in Australia. They loosed off a volley of shots and retreated into their own dust cloud. The wounded camel, though, was left weaving from left to right, its head sawing up and down, uttering a noise as indescribable as that of the guard who had been hit by a stray bullet.

A tin barrel of precious water strapped to the flank of the wounded camel had also been holed, and water spurted out in shining arcs. Seeing a camel he had bred, fed, named and groomed fall to its knees, bleeding water, Moosa could barely comprehend what was happening. Comity understood, though. The world was starting to end, just as the moon had predicted. And all because of her.

Meanwhile, troopers on the other side of the train carriages, sooner than die in ignorance, dropped their own windows, to see if the ghans were attacking from the west, too. Instead of camels or ghans, they saw large numbers of naked men and women. Wearing tall stiff cowls of tree-bark that hid their heads from sight, the figures appeared unnaturally tall and alien, and were accompanied by a horrifying sound – a wowing, moaning howl as of one gigantic, unearthly beast.

Panicked young troopers (who had never left the coast before now) levelled their rifles. Grit embedded itself in their eyeballs and made it hard to take aim.

…But they fired anyway.

At the first volley, the Aboriginals melted away into the dust haze, but the soldiers dared not take their eyes off the space where they had been, despite the startled cries of the men on the other side of the train:

"She white?"

"She's dressed white."

"She's no ghan, that's for sure."

"Who?"

"Her there. See?"

Comity had got down from her pony and walked over to the wounded camel. It was the one who had delivered the piano, she was sure, and she wanted to apologize for putting it to such pains. And for getting it shot. Its flailing hoofs, the teeth champing the air, both terrified her. But the straps had to be unfastened, because the water tanks were stopping the poor beast lying down, and things need to lie down when they are hurt, don't they? She began to struggle with the leather cinch fastened under the camel's belly.

Mr. Boyce could not help himself. He had made himself responsible for the child and how could he return her to her father in a shroud? He ventured nervously forward, waving his immaculate handkerchief over his head.

"Leave the camel, Comity. Leave the camel."

"I cannot! It is the one that brought Mama's piano."

"No. No it is not." Moosa was there now, too, his silken parcel held awkwardly high above his head as he edged within range of the train and its bristling rifles. With his other arm he signalled urgently for Comity to come away, move away, get well out of range of the guns. "This camel is only one year. Small. Too small for pianos. It is true she is valuable," he added bitterly, "but she is not your piano-camel."

A shot rang out from the train: some rookie had pulled the trigger by accident.

"Is she pure Australian?" asked Comity.

"All-through Australian, yes," said Moosa, sweating pure fear.

The owner of the camel began firing his rifle in the air to express his rage. The other men of Calgo began firing too. Their outrage smelled of gun smoke. They were working themselves up to fight.

"Why are the Army shooting at us, Mr. Boyce?"

"They must think they are under attack, Comity…as they very soon may be."

The friends and the dying camel were surrounded now by a whirling maelstrom of camels and horses whose riders were all shrieking their indignation. "Moosa, I beg you," said Boyce. "Persuade your people to a calmer state of mind. Keep them from rashness!"

"What you should do," Comity suggested, "is buy the camel."

Boyce thought, at first, that she was being sentimental – childish and sentimental – but Moosa knew she was right.

"Yes! Buy the camel, Mr. Boyce. Buy the camel, please, or there will be a great deal of blood spilled!"

So Mr. Boyce set one foot on the camel's rump and planted both hands on his hips. He was not a heroic build of man, and he regretted his baggy trousers now, which failed to say, *This is a gentleman of the British-Australian Telegraph Company.* "I wish to buy this camel!" he declared to the moiling excitement of angry cameleers. "Who owns this animal? I wish to buy this camel!"

"*Dead! Dead!*" raged a turbaned rider, jabbing his rifle at the dying camel as he galloped by.

"That does not reduce my affection for it. Kindly tell the gentleman who owns it to name his price."

General Gostard, striding purposefully down the train, stopped to watch the debacle with the camel. In front of him, over the rim of the window, came the face of the train guard, using his broom to pull himself upright.

"I am hurt. Let me in, dammit," said the guard.

The General fixed him with a look of steely enthusiasm. "In shooting you, my man, the Enemy has committed an act of war. But have no fear: we shall make them pay."

"*Just get me inside, will you?*" pleaded the guard, but General Gostard was too busy planning for the battle to come.

Mr. Boyce managed to pacify the owner of the camel, but tempers were still running high. He had to convey the full facts to the men aboard the train – tell them there was no cause for shooting – persuade them to lay down their guns. He gave his new camel a consoling pat and instructed Comity to go back, get back, get well out of range. Then he took a few nervous steps towards the train, waving his handkerchief over his head.

A bullet whined past his ear. He ran briskly backwards until he collided with Comity, who had not been following his instructions. "I cannot!" he said, wringing the handkerchief between both hands till it tore. "I cannot. I cannot. I am sorry. My wife thinks I am visiting friends! …Comity, stay close to me. You must stay out of range of those fools! And *what is that infernal noise?*"

Comity cocked her head and listened to the howling, yowling, thrumming noise echoing off every surface, even the sky. "The Devil-Devil, I expect," she said matter-of-factly. And she did not follow Mr. Boyce out of range. She went in his place to talk to the Army.

She was not meaning to be deliberately disobedient. She could quite understand about Mr. Boyce having a wife. Anyway, it was not his war. He had not invented it. It was her war: she had begun it, and it was for her to make it stop. She headed towards the train, doing her "nice walking".

After every bath time, her mother had given her lessons in how to walk nicely, balancing a book on Comity's head and having her walk around the patterned edge of the turkey carpet. *Heel-side-toes. Heel-side-toes.* She tried to do it now, although there were pebbles and things that had not littered the carpet at home. When she walked over a spent bullet, she felt the heat of it through the sole of her shoe. Mama had said that walking nicely would help her grow up into a lady. Comity did not presently mind whether she grew up into a lady or a bandicoot, so long as she did not grow up into Comity-Pinny-who-had-started-a-war-and-got-lots-of-people-killed.

Then she saw the guard sitting propped up against a wheel of the train, his broom still in one hand. She gave up on *heel-side-toes* and ran over to him.

"Are you hurt? I am so sorry. Oh, I am so sorry! It's all my fault! Here, lean on me, if you want... You look like

Britannia, sitting like that, with your broom," she added, hoping he would take it as a compliment.

By this time, forty or fifty heads were stuck out of the train windows, watching her.

"You made a terrible mistake!" she told them. "There is no war! There never was."

They lifted her up through the train windows (General Gostard having ordered the train doors to be locked). And all the time that they were dusting her down, wrapping her in a gritty blanket, asking her name, she went on telling them how there was no war, and they went on saying she was "all right now, safe now".

General Gostard tugged down the blanket to blare in her face: "How many other hostages have they taken, little girl?"

"Hostages?"

He repeated it slowly, twisting his mouth into an ugly shape as he tried to make the words perfectly understandable, even to a weak-minded child. "How many people like you did the bad men in turbans take prisoner? Do you do counting? Show me on your fingers."

Every face was puckered, struggling to hear against the unearthly booming, howling noise assailing the train.

"We came here to *rescue* you," said Comity indignantly, wriggling out of the blanket. "Why are you shooting at us?"

General Gostard did not like children. He could never guess what age they were, never guess whether the small ones were boys or girls, never command their love or attention. Women and children always complicated a straightforward battle. "You may not know it yet, child, out here in the wild, but the turban men are fighting the black men."

"No they are not, sir," said a subaltern possessed of a pair of field glasses. He offered the glasses to his commanding officer, but there was really no need for them: the situation was plain for all to see.

The howling noise had stopped. The Aboriginals had circled the train and arrived among the camels, horses and rifle-wielding ghans. Instead of a pitched battle, a strange meeting was taking place. With the awkward, wary dance movements of mating brolga-birds, bushmen and Punjabis nodded and bowed to each other, offered tentative handshakes, sidled into a line and – to the dismay of three hundred staunch and bluff soldiers – actually *held hands*.

"It does not appear that they are at war, sir," said General Gostard's aide.

Annoyance shook the General. He considered himself a man of iron, with a backbone of steel and the God-given gift of command. He was, in fact, a man incapable of changing his mind.

"No! I see it now! The blighters are not at war with each other. That was not the meaning of the telegram at all! They have joined forces! They have formed an alliance against the forces of the British Commonwealth!" He parted his feet and adopted a more statuesque pose. "Our peril is the greater, but so is the opportunity for gallantry, by God! Your country is relying on you, men! If we must, we shall fight to the last man!"

CHAPTER TWENTY-THREE

Comity

The train carriages sagged lopsidedly as a hundred troopers crossed to one side of the train and struggled to find space enough to level and fire a gun.

"No!" cried Comity, not once but twenty times. "No. You are stupid! There is no war!" But it was as if she was invisible, mute or wedged tight in a nightmare. When the trooper put her down to ready his gun, she broke free and climbed out through one of the open windows. Rolling under the train, she disturbed an assortment of lizards. Emerging on the other side of the tracks, she stood up under a thatch of serried gun barrels all clashing and clattering for want of space.

"*Stop it! Do not shoot! Please!*" she yelled, jumping up at the gun barrels, pushing at them with her fingertips. "*Go back! Go back!*" she shouted towards the friendly display of comradeship and harmony.

Though outnumbered eight-to-one, the Kinkindele mob and the Calgo cameleers were so affronted by their efforts going to waste that suddenly there really was every chance they might truly join forces to avenge the insult. The mob discarded their collars of tree bark, the ghans checked what ammunition they had. An Aboriginal family appeared carrying a length of ripped-up rail from the track. *No going back from here* was the message.

Moosa and Fred ran forward to meet Comity. They would have offered covering fire had either of them been armed. The fact that they were not armed did not stop the jittery troopers loosing off a dozen bullets in their direction. Moosa pitched on his face. Fred, a boy who had been shot two months before, lost all power of speech or movement or thought, and froze to the spot.

Comity's sprint came to an abrupt halt. She turned back to face the train. For one thing, she dared not look to see if Moosa was dead; for another she had friends to shield from the consequences of her wickedness. *You leave your friends as a camel leaves dung*, Moosa had said. Well, she would not leave them now. She would stand between the guns and her friends and make herself as big as a house. She had done a monstrous thing; well, now she would be as big as a monster, as unstoppable as a Kadimakara. Fred's ancestors, when they were finally too tired, turned themselves into mountains and trees and rocks. She would be as big as a mulga tree, as flinty as rock. She would shut her eyes and rise above it all, and be like the angels when they got out all their six wings and their unspellable names as long as the Flinders Mountains. She would *be* the Flinders Mountains. She would summon back the sea that had once rolled over Australia! When water drops began spitting in her face, it did not even surprise her. She did not even trouble to open her eyes.

But when something touched her outstretched hand, it made her jump: a dry, withered knuckly hand. Another, smoother and larger, closed round her other hand. She could hear fast, pent breathing and could not tell if it was hers or someone else's. She was too busy resolving to be like Broad in the fairy tale, who drank up the sea for the sake of his motley friends… For once in her life she would live up to her name. She would be…

"Comity!"

The shout came from way to her left, but galloped through her head from left to right; it had always been a very gallopy kind of a name – comity-comity-comity –

though she had never heard it quite so often before, nor set to the music of hoofbeats.

Scared soldiers aboard the train strained to see whether their volley of bullets had hit anything, and to make sense of the thudding hoofbeats they could hear. A galloping horse was sending stone gibber flying in all directions as it passed close along the side of the train. The troopers only glimpsed the rider as he passed directly in front of them. And they were packed so tightly together that they could not swivel their rifles to follow him. In fact, the stick he was wielding clattered along their rifle barrels and knocked them askew. A few fell clean out of their owners' startled hands. And when the rider reached the end of the train, he turned and came back again. Despite the meagre, dust-clogged daylight, his weapon flashed and flickered.

"Put up! Put up! Put up!" he yelled breathlessly. "Put up, you heathen sanguineous men!"

The stick, in error, hit a trigger finger, and a rifle went off, right alongside the horse's head. The horse sheared away from the train in terror and put the rider in plain view of the whole train. Those who had thought the stick tipped with fire saw that it was in fact a crystal-topped walking cane, and that the knight's clothes were all wrong for riding. The trousers were so tight that they had ridden up to his knees. The shoes were city shoes. The dapper waistcoat had lost all its buttons in the exertion. The sleeves had come adrift from the suit jacket. His horse's fright had made the rider lose his stirrups and he was clinging to its neck, halfway to being unhorsed. A dozen troopers, nerves taut as piano wire, burst into giggles at the sight.

General Gostard did not so much as smile. He raised his pistol.

As the deafened horse turned in agitated circles, shaking its head, its ears crackled. The noise was duplicated by raindrops falling on the metal carriage roof. Huge raindrops, as big as bullets.

"Desist in this ungodly belligerence!" The horseman's voice was high and reedy with fright; it increased the laughter. But as Herbert Pinny recovered control of both his mount and his voice, and Horse came plodding and blowing towards the train again, the laughter faded away. There was a furious dignity about the man, who held over his head a small slip of white.

General Gostard took aim. "Halt or I fire!"

"Sir, I must protest!" said his aide. "The man is under a flag of parley!" And he actually tugged the pistol out of his commanding officer's hand and threw it on the bunk.

"I have here a telegram recalling you to barracks!" shouted the rider. "Had you reached Oodnadatta, you would have learned the situation there. Since you became stranded, you weltered in ignorance and thirst. Your fellow countrymen were obliged to seek you out with water and relief."

Like a burdi drawing in its claws, the troop train withdrew three hundred rifles from its windows. In their place, six hundred cupped hands reached out to catch the falling rain.

The rain cleared the air of dust. The telegram laid the dust of misunderstanding. The train doors were unlocked and Herbert Pinny was invited to come aboard. The fellahs separated from the cameleers of Calgo Crossing without a word spoken, and the two groups drifted apart.

Only one row of figures remained standing in the open, like paper dollies cut from a single sheet of newspaper. Comity, Fred, Moosa, Loud Lulu and Mr. Boyce stood, arms outstretched, hand-in-hand. Not until Pinny signalled to them from the steps of the train did they glance at one another, kiss whatever hand they were holding, and let go.

CHAPTER TWENTY-FOUR

Lies...

Even dismounted from Horse, even though he stood only as tall as the General's shoulder, Herbert Pinny seemed a large enough threat for the aide to step between them while he read the telegram.

"It does appear, sir, that we are recalled, as this gentleman said. There is no truth in the rumour of a war."

Herbert Pinny reached past him and struck Gostard on the chest with the back of his hand. "And yet you were ready to fire on women and children in your lust for pomp!"

"Pomp? Pomp?" honked the General, struggling to hear above the drumming of the rain, struggling to read the wet telegram his aide had just handed him. He did not have his reading glasses. He was also allergic to being in the wrong. "May I remind you, sir, that I represent the Queen, the will of the Nation and the preservation of Law!"

"And may I remind *you*, sir, that I represent Communication and the free passage of intelligence – two things you would appear singularly to lack!"

"There are abos under the train, sir!" called a trooper from the next carriage. "Do we mind abos under the train?"

"*Why? Would you prefer them to stand out in the rain?*" Pinny yelled back, leaving General Gostard, mouth open to speak, looking like a hooked cod.

"Pinny, old chap," called Jack Boyce from the foot of the train steps, "it is damp out here. Do you have room for one or two more?" He lifted Comity up into the carriage and her father, face as thunderous as Jove, grabbed her by the dress and pulled her violently up against him, his arm so tight around her that she thought he was about to denounce her then and there: the Girl Who Had Started the War.

"This," said Herbert Pinny, "is my daughter. My flesh and blood. My solitary joy in this torpid world. And would you SHOOT her? Without a question asked? Without knowing her reason for standing before you? These, her friends – would you shoot them because when they arrived to rescue your sorry hide, they were wearing a *different colour skin?"*

Troopers were slowly encroaching on the officers' carriage to listen in, jostling so close together that their kit made a noise like a herd of spiny anteaters.

"A war was reported!" Backed up against his unmade bunk, General Gostard took his stand. "A war was reported! Words emanated from the telegraphic station at Kikundilly that... These things do not happen by accident!"

Mauled and pulled about by the ferocity of her father's left hand, Comity felt the very moment at which his anger ran out. He took the hand away and looked at its palm, wet and plastered with strands of her hair. The hand shook.

Comity mustered her courage – which was a little bit spent, what with being a six-winged seraphim and Broad and a Kadimakara and a mountain range all in the space of five minutes. She knew what she must say.

Please, sir (she must say) *I sent the message about the war, to stop my cousins coming, because I told them lies and I did not want them to find out.*

It was very important that she did not mention her mother dying or Papa's...difficulties. Or the dead people in the yard. That way, no one need ever go to Kinkindele, or blame Papa for being bullied by the stars and Mr. Hogg. It would not be difficult to speak up, not after being called flesh-and-blood and a solitary joy. Not hard at all. Let the Army take her back to Adelaide and put her in prison. Ten years from now, her father would come and collect her from the prison gate, because she was a solitary joy and flesh-and-blood.

"Please, sir, I—"

Herbert Pinny's hand flew out again. Grabbing her entire head, he drew her face against his chest. Through his waistcoat she heard him say, "I myself accept full—"

Jumping up the steep steps and shaking himself like a wet dog, nice Mr. Boyce erupted into the carriage, racked by a fit of the noisiest coughing. "I think *I* may shed light on this extraordinary turn of events," he said, speaking uncharacteristically loudly. And taking a damp notepad and pencil from his inner pocket, he began to draw rows of neat perforated lines, holding the pad up against the wall of the carriage. "This, you see, is the original message, as it was despatched from Kinkindele Repeater Station Number Four. *DO NOT COME STOP REGRET NATIVES AND CALGO GANS AT* . . . And now we come to it."

General Gostard, his aide and three other officers peered over his shoulder at the smudged chain-link of dots and dashes.

"And now we come to it, gentlemen… I take it you all read Morse?" (They would not, they *must* not. Everything depended on it.)

General Gostard uttered a snort of contempt for all codes, Morse in particular. Three of the other officers turned away, defeated. But one captain remained at Boyce's shoulder. "As a boy I mastered it, yes sir."

And Boyce's lie fell apart, along with the notepad in his grasp. Ninety squares of paper fluttered from between its covers and onto the floor of the carriage. As he bent to pick them up, Moosa and Fred went down on their knees to help. Their heads touched. Words were spoken, though with barely a sound. Moments later, Boyce was up on his feet again.

$$\bullet\,-\,-\,/\,\bullet\,-\,/\,\bullet\,-\,\bullet$$

he wrote in giant, fierce dots and dashes that tore the page he was writing on. "W-A-R…" he translated. Then moved on to another sheet.

$$\bullet\,-\,\bullet\,/\,-\,-\,-\,/\,-\,\bullet\,\bullet\,\bullet\,/\,-\,-\,-\,/\,\bullet\,-\,\bullet\,/\,\bullet\,/\,\bullet$$

he wrote triumphantly. "R-O-B-O-R-E-E."

"W-A-R-R-O-B-O-R-E-E," said the Captain-who-knew-Morse. "Warroboree?"

"Warroboree?" said General Gostard.

"Warroboree?" said several bewildered voices. "What does it mean?"

"Warroboree! An Aboriginal word, sir," said Moosa. "A festival of story and singing and general jollity."

All eyes turned on Fred for confirmation. After all, how would a ghan know anything of the Aboriginal language? It was a well-known fact – well, up until today it had been a well-known fact – that the two races hated each other.

"Warroboree. Yay. Verily. Byallmean," said Fred. "Big singalong. Stories. Magic with loaves and fishes. Turkey on a spit." Lying had always been his particular genius.

Jack Boyce briefly closed his eyes and ran both palms over his skull, smoothing his splendid grey hair into place. "Who knows what caused the glitch, gentlemen? A momentary fault on the Wire…a bolt of lightning, a wild hog scratching itself against a telegraph pole, a thieving… *magpie* stealing one of the porcelain insulators… Such tiny mishaps are all it takes to interrupt transmission. Thus the final letters of the message were lost. WARROBOREE was reduced to a mere three-letter stub. FESTIVAL became WAR and a tiny mishap was turned to near-tragedy. No one's fault, but a dashed close call, eh, gentlemen?"

There was a moment's silence in the carriage, which made Comity want to clap and clap and clap and throw flowers onstage, even though she had never been to the theatre in her life.

Then, as the eavesdropping troopers passed the word along, and news of the ridiculous "mistake" ran forward along the train, the sound of laughter grew so loud that it drowned out the rain squall. It even reached the Calgo camels, lugubriously chewing cud and flicking water off their hairy ears.

Once again, the moon had risen blood-red. In the uppermost eaves of the sky, dust scraped up hundreds of miles away still hung in the atmosphere, colouring in the moon. Cautiously, Comity broached the subject.

"Mr. Boyce says the world might *not* be going to end."

"I do not suppose it is for one moment, dearest," said her father. He tasted some of the meat Fred had cooked them over the bonfire at their camp. "This is good. What is it?"

"Don't ask," advised Jack Boyce. "Sometimes it is best not to ask."

This harmless truth hung in the air like smoke from the fire: sometimes it is best not to ask what the future holds in store. But Comity had an aching need to know: *was* the world about to end – her world, the world of Kinkindele?

Her father answered her unspoken question.

"I shall be punished, Comity. How could I not be? Six people lie dead in the yard, because I failed to keep order on my own station. When Hogg shot Fred, strangers saved him, not I."

"But you did not even know he had been shot, old man..."

"Then I *should* have known, Jack. I should not have been locked in a back room, quacking like a one-legged duck."

Boyce shook his head so hard that he rocked on his haunches. "Extenuating circumstances, man. You were ill. Hogg seized his moment!"

"Ill?" Herbert looked reproachfully at his old friend. "Ill?"

Comity had devoted a lot of thought to this. Words are important. They are like things you throw when the stove catches fire. Some put the fire out. Some make the whole house burn down. "Brain fever," she suggested. "In Mama's novels, people are always getting brain fever. Men and women."

"You read Mama's novels?"

"No, but she used to tell me the plots after she read them, and many, many people got brain fever and no one thought bad of them for it."

Herbert smiled ruefully. "And what became of all these fevered people?"

"They died, or they got saved by the love of a good woman."

In a way, it was quite as awful a thing to say as telling a story about the Great Snake Ancestor at the dinner table just when snakes were the most unmentionable thing in the world. *The love of a good woman* was something lost to them both for ever. But tonight, from all around them in the dark came a crackling sound of parakeelya plants and desert peas absorbing the brief rain, spreading, swelling, reaching out shoots. Tomorrow the ground would be cloaked in a coat of purple and red. For a little while the whole landscape would be a riot of brightness. Tonight, even the truth was allowed.

Herbert found on his plate some recognizable animal part that made him set his dinner aside. "Do not make excuses for me, my love. The piper must be paid. As soon as we are home, I shall write an accurate account of events and send it to the Superintendent, along with my resignation."

Comity caught her breath. A fear went through her so shrill and clamorous that for the first time, she caught a glimpse of what her father felt when he saw the stars massing. She realized she was afraid – petrified – of leaving Kinkindele and its edgeless, circling emptiness. What, leave Fred when she had only just got him back? Live in the real world rather than inside the shelter she had built of stories, fantasies? It made her stomach cramp and her throat close and puffballs of darkness swell and explode inside her eyelids. She must rise above it – the embroidery on the wall at Telegraph House said so. But go to Adelaide? To a home with no machine room? To live without the rattle of Morse peppering her days and nights with letters? It would be like losing her own heartbeat. Her mother was buried at Kinkindele! Must they leave her there, alone in the ground, with strangers walking over her grave? Comity felt sick and sweaty and helpless and filleted of all grown-upness.

"Oh please, Father! Do not tell Superintendent Bligh I called his children noxious!"

"Well no, naturally I shall be selective in what I say…"

"Well then, Henry old chap," Mr. Boyce broke in, "while you are 'being selective', could you not mention my part in this? Or I too will have to resign. Selfish, I know, but I love my work."

"I know that, Jack…"

"And selfishness aside…Fred and Moosa might also pay dear for helping me out in my lie back there."

"Oh, I think—" began Herbert.

"Also, if they jail you, your girl will certainly be thrown on the mercy of the Bligh family."

"Oh, Father!"

Fred dodged lightly in from the shadows to retrieve the leftover lizard. He took the opportunity to say in Comity's ear, in a stage whisper, "If your old man go to prison, you come live in my gunyah."

Herbert Pinny studied the boy crouching by his daughter, a half-eaten lizard in his hand. As they healed, the muscles in Fred's chest had knitted up shorter than before, so that one scarred shoulder was raised higher than the other. Suddenly the red moon overhead was a bullet wound in a black chest, reproaching Herbert for his uselessness. That Fred should offer to take care of his daughter was the greatest reproach of all. Pinny felt his hands begin to shake, his back teeth to grind. Overhead the stars were sharpening themselves to points, taking aim on him... Perhaps Comity would be better off with her cousins in Adelaide.

"How did you get here, Pa?" asked Comity suddenly. "Fred's got magic ancestors to help. But how did you manage it? With the stars looking, and all."

The question took him unawares. "What do you mean, girl? How could I not?"

*

Herbert remembered struggling up out of the treacly trance Comity had put him in with her pituri juice; remembered swimming up towards daylight, like a wasp in a tin of syrup. He remembered the sound of Jack Boyce and Comity discussing him.

"The first thing I heard as I woke was my daughter's voice, explaining why she had drugged me. For fear I would murder her. What horror could the world hold for me after that? Kill my daughter? How could she think that? I am her father! From the day she was born, it was for me to keep her safe. Throw myself bodily on snakes! Hold open the jaws of wild dogs with my bare hands. Drink up floods if necessary. If the Flinders Mountains take it into their heads to stampede over the desert now, this minute, it is for me to head them off! Is her mother dead? Then I must be mother and father to her! Is every nation in the world at war? Then I must bang their heads together and send them to their rooms. Is Australia on fire? Then I must tie a line to it and tow it to Antarctica behind a rowing boat, and douse it with snow! What horror compares with NOT keeping my daughter safe?

"So I cursed myself, as I deserved to be cursed, and I wrapped my head in that curse, as Moosa there binds his, and I came along after you. And when my demons came out to threaten me, I shouted them down. *Want to pelt me, do you, stars? I'll blow you out like candles. Those walls of rock waiting to clash on me like cymbals – let them. I've felt worse. Look, that cheese-wire horizon waiting to slice off my head – wait your turn: there are people ahead of you in the queue with better reasons. Sky, you want to stifle me like a bird in a bell jar? Try it: I can hold my breath as long as it takes. As long as it takes to see my girl safe again. You faceless things in the shadows, come round where I can see you and I'll spit in your eye! You cannot be uglier than what I see when I look in the shaving mirror. Let God desert me, before I ever let her down again…*

"And you know what? They held off. They thought twice. I suppose they had never seen a monster as great as me. A father whose daughter fears he might murder her and bury her in the yard? That's horror enough to sour the Milky Way."

The eaves of the sky were emptying of dust. Soon the moon wore only a vestige of red, like a blush in both cheeks. The stars, like flocking galahs, seemed a hopeful, cheerful sign of life. Herbert Pinny's hands stopped shaking. His heart expanded, as parakeelya flowers do after a shower of rain.

"You ever do awake-dreaming, Pa Pinny?" asked Fred. It was outrageously impertinent. It was cheeky beyond belief.

"Fred!" said Comity.

But Mr. Pinny was not offended. "Sometimes I pretend Mrs. Pinny is still alive. Out of the room, merely. Topping up a battery. Or putting a splint on a chicken's leg. Or sewing her quilt."

"Splendid first-rate," said Fred. He looked over at Moosa and asked the same question. Moosa shook his head: he did not do daydreaming.

"Yes you do, Moosa," said Comity. "You dream of the Governor of Australia sitting down to breakfast and saying 'Bring me some of Moosa Rasul's excellent date marmalade!'"

"How do you know this?" said Moosa, sitting bolt upright.

Nice Mr. Boyce cleared his throat. "I confess that sometimes I pretend I stole Mary Triggers from Herbert Pinny on the day of their wedding, and eloped with her to Tasmania on a fishing boat. I do apologize old chap, but she really was the sweetest girl in Adelaide. I know I never stood a chance beside you, but one can dream."

"The Missus liked stories bigly," said Fred, sly as a dingo. "We should to make up story special for the Missus. Make her happy."

They turned to look at him, skinny, frail and gawky as a joey fallen from a kangaroo's pouch.

"Fred Waters, you are the Tempter in the Garden of Eden," said Herbert Pinny.

Fred nibbled on his lizard contentedly. "Sorry? Pagan me. Not know Bible, me. Verily."

That night they put together a story between them. Not an ancient tale, old as the world, such as you might hear at a corroboree. This was a new story. A story of what might have been.

It was the story of a terrible illness. An illness that struck down six good men and the Stationmaster's wife in the course of a single night. The Stationmaster only survived because he happened to be away from home, preventing a war.

Seven well-tended graves look much like seven graves newly dug. Who was to say when those in the graves had died, or what had killed them? ...Well, to be honest, any one of the stockmen or cameleers could have told. But they would not. They would not put the lie to Herbert Pinny's story. Both Aboriginal and ghan can swallow secrets, as the desert swallows rain.

The British-Australian Telegraph Company were appalled by the news of seven sudden deaths at Kinkindele. They sent their most profound regrets. Herbert sent his own, to the families of Amos and Hart and Cage and Smith and Sankey, couched in words as raw and grief-filled as if their deaths had happened only hours before. The pain, after all, had been weighing on his conscience for months, heavy as a piano.

Nice Mr. Boyce confided nothing to his wife of what he had found at Kinkindele, and not much about the excitements that had followed. He had a feeling that, if he did tell her, she would never let him put on baggy trousers and go upcountry again to sleep under the stars.

When, one day, local carriers delivered a lame camel to his door, he smothered his astonishment, read the letter that came with the delivery – *Your purchase, sir. The sweets prevailed. Allah is good. Moosa Rasul* – and told his wife that the camel was a gift from an old friend.

His wife wanted to butcher it for camel steak, but Mr. Boyce widened his eyes at her in a way that silenced her instantly. He fenced off a paddock and bought a donkey as company for his pet camel.

CHAPTER TWENTY-FIVE

...and Truths

The Blighs did come to Kinkindele. Shaken by the shocking news of all those deaths at Station Four, Aunt Berenice felt obliged to visit her sister's grave and to make Herbert Pinny feel the full weight of her family's disappointment in him. She brought her children too, of course, their suitcases full of contempt and smugness. Alexander, Anne and Albert looked around them from the steps of the carriage, lips curled with disdain. Just as they had thought: no fountains, no pony jumps, no emus roosting on the roof, no dam.

"Goodness! You never believed all that, did you?" said Comity with a happy, hiccupping little laugh. "In your letters you seemed to be having such a dull time. I thought you needed some stories to cheer you up."

Someone else in the carriage was slower to get down – someone so frail and black-clad that, in the dark interior, she could have been mistaken for a forgotten umbrella.

"You are Grandma Triggers," Comity said in astonishment, and helped her down the steps. Here was a worrying surprise: the Blighs had announced their coming, but they had said nothing of bringing Mary's mother too. In her panic, Comity could not remember: how long was it since she had written to her grandmother? What nonsense had she last invented while pretending Mary Pinny was still alive? What and when (if ever) had Grandma Triggers written back?

"How is the knitting?" Comity asked, to stave off any subject more upsetting. "I knit, look." And she pulled free the knitting needles that were fastening up her hair.

"Arthritis forbids it these days, my dear," said the old lady, fingering the coil of hair that had fallen onto Comity's shoulder. "Just the colour of Mary's," she said. "…And how is Ivanhoe?"

They were standing where the washing had once hung, Comity almost on the spot where the wash basket had stood, where Hogg's pitch-and-toss stones had cracked together, where she had dragged her mother's window boxes so as to prop up grave boards and keep the ghosts away.

"I made Ivanhoe up," said Comity.

"I know."

How strange. It must be inherited. Her mother had had it. And Mary must have inherited it from *her* mother: the art of reading between the lines.

"I knew from your very first letter… Do you suppose a mother does not know when her own daughter… I suppose you wished to spare me pain?"

"Yes," said Comity. "And no."

She hoped it was inherited – that she had inherited it – that thing both mother and grandmother could do (apart from knitting): the art of saying things without speaking them out loud.

"I would have come before. But the sadness of it… made me unwell. Sadness can do that, Comity."

"I know. Brain fever. It did that to Papa."

"Ah. And is he recovered?"

"Oh yes, quite recovered, almost." She looked at her grandmother – tried to look and look and look her words clear into the old lady's head: *Do not say Mama has been dead for a year. Do not give him away. Do not call him a liar.* "Well, Mama has been gone only a few weeks, Grandma, but we are trying to be brave."

"Of course," said Grandma Triggers. "Of course."

The others were calling to them from the verandah. Aunt Berenice was sending the children back to chivvy their grandmother.

"One day soon we shall have a good talk about it. And you can tell me it all. Exactly as it happened?"

"Yes, of course! Naturally!" said Comity. "Soon. One day. Of course. Yes. Probably. Possibly."

At dinner the subject arose, of course, of Comity returning to Adelaide to live with the Blighs.

"I need her with me," said Herbert. "She is my great abiding joy."

"We need each other," said Comity.

Aunt Berenice shifted irritably in her chair and frowned at Comity for interrupting a conversation between adults. "Yes, but we must not be selfish at a time like this, Herbert. Look at the child. She is barely civilized. Why, you are not even able to dress her in mourning for her own mother!"

"For whom should we wear it? Each other?" enquired Herbert. "We have no need to remind each other of what we have lost."

The Bligh children smirked at Comity across the table. Anne crooked her little finger as she lifted her teacup, to show how civilized she was herself. "You may live with us if you care to, Comity. I can teach you how to play the piano." "Pi-ar-no" was how she said it. "I am very gifted at the pi-ar-no, you know."

Anne's brothers glared at her. They did not want another girl in the house: one was bad enough. Alexander hurriedly suggested, "She would probably be too scared to live in the city. She would not know how to use a knife and fork – or flush a real toilet."

Comity looked at them thoughtfully for a moment or two before leaning forward as if to confide a secret. "I *will* go back to Adelaide one day. Not yet, but I will go back. I mean to train as a Morse operator." Her father dropped his soup spoon. Her grandmother merely inclined her head and declared it "an interesting and useful profession".

"Girls cannot do that," said Albert flatly. "They are too feather-brained. Father says. And *he* is Superintendent of Telegraphs."

Comity helped herself to a little more date chutney. "In that case, I shall go to Scotland," she said, "where Grandpa came from. I heard it is more civilized than Adelaide. So the Superintendents might be cleverer."

Aunt Berenice had no chance to give her a telling-off before Alexander gave a hoggish snort of laughter: "What and leave poor 'Prince Frederick'? You would break poor

Prince Frederick's heart! Or did he go out sailing and get drowned in *the Sea*?" It was said so snidely that even Aunt Berenice was embarrassed and scowled at her three children, snickering and sniggering into their hands.

Comity blushed. The parlour seemed unpleasantly full, stifling and oppressive. Luckily, her grandmother answered for her.

"Oh, and do you care to see the Sea, children? I believe Prince Frederick may be in Prussia at present, buying cossacks, but I am sure Comity could take you there this afternoon. Mary wrote of it in her letters and I confess I was intrigued. I am only sorry my old bones are not equal to the walk."

"I am sorry too, Grandma. I would like to have shown you," said Comity, with a graciousness so like her mother that Herbert and Grandma Triggers exchanged a bittersweet glance.

Confused and resentful, the Bligh children fell in behind Comity who, in her new boots and armed with her father's walking cane, walked so fast that they had to trot to keep up.

"Why do you wear ditting deedles in your hair?" said Albert through swollen adenoids.

"They are my totem," said Comity. "Our stockmen have a bandicoot totem. In the Dreamtime their ancestor was a bandicoot. Mine knitted."

"And what, pray, is a bandicoot?" gasped Anne, breathless and sweating. But she lost interest in the answer as she caught sight of her first scorpion.

Already Comity had pointed out a rat-like thing as big as a rabbit, horned beetles, fleshy white grubs, and one bird butchering another bird in the vilest way imaginable. Introduced to a carnivorous plant, Albert had tried to push Anne's finger into its funnel of poison, so she was not speaking to him any more. Alexander had demanded to see where the camel had kicked Comity, and sunk into a sulk when she was able to show him the scar.

"Is it much farther?" he said now. "This walking is *tedious*." He was doing his best to appear rugged and bored, but the swirls of spinifex grass had sawtooth edges and he had brushed his ankles against so many that he urgently wanted to cry. "I cannot hear *seagulls*," he added sarcastically.

"Oh!" Comity put her hands to her chest and gasped with theatrical alarm. "I hope you are not expecting waves and fishing boats! That would be absurd! The ocean dried up an age ago. Before Noah died, I should think."

Then she went on to show them ammonites and

seashells, skeletons of fish as delicate as tiny harps; the teeth of shark and the fronded ghosts of coral-plumes preserved for ever inside the rocks.

The galling notion began to grow in the Blighs that their cousin was neither mad nor a fibber. What with the frightening things she seemed to know, and the torrent of local stories she loosed over them – "…*and then one day a flood of nectar washed the bandicoots out of hell and into a mulga thicket…*" – they barely dared to query anything that spilled from her mouth. After all, standing on a seabed in the Middle of Nowhere makes almost anything possible.

But little Albert saw his chance at last, when Comity showed them the Aboriginal paintings in the caves beside the dry sea. He drew from his pocket a purse of coloured crayons and declared that he could do better.

"No. These are sacred pictures, Albert," said Comity. "They have magic."

"They're puny," said Albert. "The people dot got faces. I'm going to give them eyes and ears!"

"No. You must not. Truly," said Comity, as firmly as she knew how.

The Blighs smelled blood. "They are rude. They need clothes," said Anne. "Give them some clothes, Albert."

"And a carriage to go about in," said Alexander, grinning.

"And a house with curtains!"

"There are handprints, look. We should all leave our handprints!"

"*They are a thousand years old*," Comity insisted. "They were painted by the ancestors. You would not crayon in a church, would you?" But she could hear the panic in her voice and see the dingo glint in their eyes. She should never have brought them here, should never have been tempted to show Fred's secrets to the noxious Blighs. Alexander and Albert began crayoning the palms of their hands, ready to make handprints. Albert drew out a red crayon and leaned one hand on the cave wall. A dingo-pink tongue poked out of the side of his small mouth as he prepared to improve on the sacred paintings.

Then a drone, like wind among buildings.

"What's that?" said Anne, spinning round.

The drone throbbed and sobbed, louder and louder, passing in and out of a musical note found nowhere on any piano keyboard. It thrummed as if there might be feathers attached to whatever was making it – wings – a sting, even. Urging and surging and circling and swooping, it seemed to surround them, its echo filling the cave as a howl fills a dog's gullet.

Albert dropped his crayons. Alexander and Anne looked at Comity for her to say something reassuring.

Her face was as coldly blank as any of the painted warriors' on the wall. "What did you expect?" she said. "Now you have roused up the *guardian monsters*."

The Blighs ran so fast they had no breath left for screaming. The only noise to escape them was a sporadic squeak and squeal, as of piglets rolling down a hillside.

Fred appeared from nowhere, wrapping the bullroarer round and round with its string. For weeks he had been promising to show one to Comity: ever since the War of Calgo Spur Line. She had doubted his promise, knowing full well that bullroarer magic was not meant for girls – nor for little boys uninitiated into the mysteries of manhood. But here he was, pressing the magic noise-maker into her hand – an oval of wattle wood etched and stained with patterns.

"You made it?" she said. "It's beautiful."

"Against Regulations. I am not man yet. You better have it."

"Me?" said Comity. "What, always?"

"Byallmean," said Fred.

"Verily?"

"Verily."

He took her other hand and pressed it to the wall alongside the palm-prints of his ancestors. Spread against the rock, his own hand was smaller than hers.

Neither left a print: that was not the intention. It was more as if the two of them were stroking the flank of a great beast – feeling its red heart beat through the smoothness of its ancient hide.

The End

A Guide to Comity's World

*allinger yerra-bamalla** it is sunset

*Altjeringa **   the land of the Dreamtime;
the land of Byamee

*arcoona **   it's no good

Big Red   a (red) kangaroo

brolga bird   the delicate and dancing
Australian crane

*bulyakarak **   spiritually powerful person

burdi   a burrowing rat-kangaroo

comity   courtesy, especially between
nations who respect each other's
laws and customs

coolabah	a kind of eucalyptus tree
corella	a long-billed cockatoo
corroboree *	tribal gathering with dance and storytelling
cull-la *	all right
dillybag	small bag woven from plant fibres or grass and worn round the neck to carry gathered food or tools
djanak *	spirit being
Dreamtime	a legendary Aboriginal age during which the world was created and shaped, and the ancestors (both human and animal) introduced the skill and customs needed for day-to-day living
galah	a kind of parrot
ghan	a native of Afghanistan or India,

encouraged to bring to Australia
his camels and his experience of
delivering goods by camel trains.
Camels were ideally suited to the
harsh, dry Australian outback

ghantown   settlements built by the ghans

goanna   a large lizard

goonawodli *   toilet

gunyah *   camp or shelter

jacky   used in the past by non-Aboriginals
to refer to Aboriginal males
regardless of their actual name

jerky   beef cut into strips and dried in
the sun

Kadimakara   an Aboriginal term for monsters
who lived during the Dreamtime
and, when the trees disappeared,
wandered in the desert until they

died, leaving only their bones. Hence the name given by archaeologists to a unique breed of dinosaur identified from a single find of skull fragments

kardang *	little brother
kert-kert *	quickly
koppi unga *	give me some water
korr *	come back
kubang *	friend
kulpernatoma *	I'm talking to you
kurlang *	son/child
lilly-pilly *	a myrtle tree or rose apple
Macassar oil	a preparation used by men to keep their hair plastered in place

malka karak *	doctor
mantanekin *	wait for me
min-min *	floating lights sometimes glimpsed in the Outback a natural phenomenon
mob	Aboriginal term for family or clan or group
mulga	an acacia tree, its wood often used in house building
Mullah	used in the past by non-Muslims as a name for any ghan settler; in fact a Muslim teacher or authority in Islamic law – a figure of authority within any community
ngai ouri *	come here
perentie lizard	a huge flesh-eating lizard, the biggest in Australia, growing to over two metres in length

pituri	a shrubby tree, also the juice made from its leaves, used by huntsmen to drug and slow down fast-moving emu
spencer	a short vest
spinifex	sharp-pointed Australian grass, sometimes called porcupine grass
stockmen	farmhands (usually Aboriginal) who looked after cattle
thrunkkun *	go away
tintown	same as ghantown, so-called because of the use of sheet metal in the buildings
wayarn *	afraid
wija narani *	I am leaving
windana? *	which way?

witchetty grubs	larvae of a moth or beetle
woomera	a stick used to propel a spear
yamble *	a lie or tall story
yarrura? *	what am I going to do?
yirra *	up

*All words marked with * are Aboriginal words from the Pama-Nyungan dialect.*

Author's Note

Authors invent more than just characters and plots. They invent settings too, whether it's an ocean-going liner or a distant planet. Even when a book is set in a place with a real map reference, road numbers and postcodes, its depiction in a book will only be like a reflection in a lake – warped and rumpled by the author's every sigh.

So you could travel the whole length of The Wire, from Australia's south coast to north, and you wouldn't find any trace of the telegraph repeater station at Kinkindele – or even of Kinkindele: they do not exist, any more than Comity or Fred or Herbert or Hogg exist. Nor does Calgo Crossing, or the spur railway that sheers off towards it from the old Oodnadatta Track.

This is a shocking liberty to take with someone else's country, especially when it is the country which inspired me to write the book! But although, while I was there, I drank in as much as I could – though I travelled the same journey as a telegram, from south coast to north, and flew in a hot air balloon over the russet landscape – I cannot possibly claim to *know* the place. Australia is a thousand countries tacked together by rivers and mountains. Its myths are as countless and varied as its birds. Its people are as varied as...well, as people anywhere. So I dipped my nib into fact to write this book, but mostly I dipped it into my imagination.

It would be even more of a liberty to pretend I knew all about the cultural and spiritual life of a Punjabi cameleer or an Aboriginal stockman. But Fred has grown up under the influences of two cultures – so has Moosa. They are not "cultural types" but unique products of everything that's happened to them, everyone they've met. (We all are.)

The other far-off place I like my writing to take me is the Past – an *entirely* different country, where people thought differently, behaved differently and carried different memories in their heads. In the nineteenth century – and not just in Australia – different nationalities hated, despised and mistrusted each other. I would like to say that 120 years of progress have changed all that.

I would *like* to say that.

As I write this, there seems to be a more urgent need than ever for "comity" – harmony and understanding between nations. ...But then, if real life could achieve happy endings as easily as stories can, there might be no need for authors to invent them.

Thank you, thank you...

Like Herbert Pinny, I like working alone, filling my days up with words. But of course that's not a true picture of the writing life. Many, many people are involved in bringing a book to life, and I am hugely grateful to all of them for making this one: Rebecca for liking the idea; Anne, Sarah and Stephanie for rescuing me from my mistakes; designers Hannah and Sarah; Amy and Liz for telling people about it; author and friend Kate Forsyth; Nola Turner-Jensen, Cristina Cappelluto, Abigail Wheatley and Margaret Cole for their advice; also the excellent people I met in Australia (especially at Alice Springs) who introduced me to the world of the repeater station, the Ghan railway and the camel trains.

I must acknowledge my debt to R Lewis and H W Reed whose lexicons of Aboriginal language and collection of myths I was all too dependent on.

Thank you, too, to the ghosts of all those remarkable and motley inhabitants of the nineteenth-century Red Heart, whose footprints smoothed the harsh path to modern-day Australia.

About the Author

GERALDINE McCAUGHREAN is one of today's most successful and highly regarded children's authors. She has won the Carnegie Medal, the Whitbread Children's Book Award three times, the Guardian Children's Fiction Prize, the Smarties Bronze Award four times, the prestigious U.S. Printz Award and the Blue Peter Book of the Year Award. She was chosen to write the official sequel to J. M. Barrie's *Peter Pan*, *Peter Pan in Scarlet* which was published to wide critical acclaim.

Geraldine lives in Berkshire with her husband, John, and the lingering shades of all those characters she has invented in her books.

www.geraldinemccaughrean.co.uk

also available

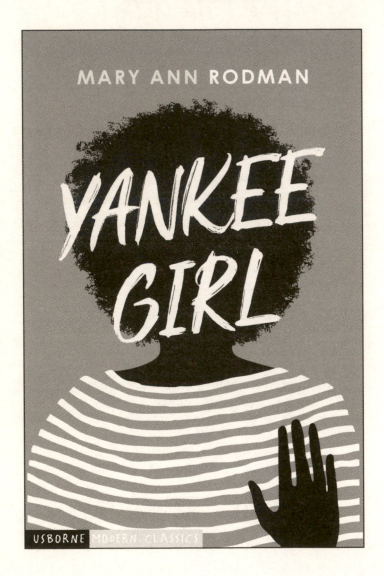

MARY ANN RODMAN

YANKEE GIRL

USBORNE MODERN CLASSICS

It's 1964 and Alice has moved to Mississippi from
Chicago with her family. Nicknamed 'Yankee Girl'
and taunted by the in-crowd at school, Alice soon
discovers the other new girl Valerie – one of the school's
first black students – has it much worse.

Alice can't stand the way Valerie is treated,
and yet she knows she will remain an outsider
if she speaks up. It takes a horrible tragedy to
finally give Alice the courage to stand up
for what she believes.

*Set in the Deep South in the 1960s,
Yankee Girl is a powerful, resonant
and relevant story about racism and
doing the right thing.*

USBORNE MODERN CLASSICS

introducing timeless stories to today's reader

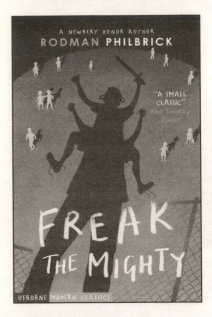

Introducing timeless stories to today's readers

PAGE-TURNER
PRIZE-WINNER

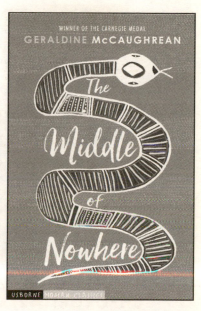

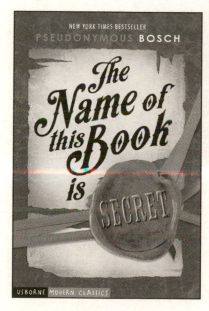

RIB-TICKLER
BEST-SELLER

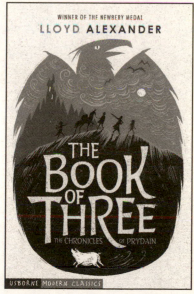

CULT CLASSIC
TIMELESS ADVENTURE